Forever and Ever and Evie

Stella Etc.

Karen McCombie

Forever and Ever and Evie

Stella Etc.

First published in the UK in 2007 by Scholastic Children's Books
An imprint of Scholastic Ltd
Euston House, 24 Eversholt Street
London, NW1 1DB, UK
Registered office: Westfield Road, Southam, Warwickshire, CV47 0RA
SCHOLASTIC and associated logos are trademarks and/or registered
trademarks of Scholastic Inc.

This edition published in the UK by Scholastic Ltd, 2011

Text copyright © Karen McCombie, 2007
The right of Karen McCombie to be identified as the author of this work
has been asserted by her.

ISBN 978 1407 12419 3

British Library Cataloguing-in-Publication Data
A CIP catalogue record for this book is available from the British Library.

Printed in the UK by CPI Bookmarque Ltd, Croydon, Surrey
Papers used by Scholastic Children's Books are made from wood grown in
sustainable forests.

1 3 5 7 9 10 8 6 4 2

This is a work of fiction. Names, characters, places, incidents and dialogues are products of
the author's imagination or are used fictitiously. Any resemblance to actual people, living or
dead, events or locales is entirely coincidental.

www.scholastic.co.uk/zone

Contents

From: *stella*
To: Frankie
Subject: **Still gobsmacked and reeling**
Attachments: **Forever And Ever & Evie**

Hi Frankie!

Kpo'k,,okppppppppppppp'p.."""""""""""""""""""[.'ppppp
ppppppppp

Sorry – that was Peaches trying to sit on the keyboard – I've shooed him off and he's gone under the desk to sulk. (I can feel his tail flicking grumpily against my ankle.)

And sorry, sorry, sorry it's taken a whole week to e-mail you, but you know how manic it gets when you start back at school after a holiday. I mean, teachers seem to expect you to work and everything!

Of course, it isn't just the seventy-five tons of homework that's been taking up brain space; it's the fact that I'm still gobsmacked and reeling. You got my text last Sunday, right? I didn't mean to blast you with news like that and then leave you hanging. So I've spent every lunchtime this week in the library, writing up everything that happened when I came to London for half-term. And

1

especially what happened right after it (since that's the bit I haven't explained properly to you yet). . .

Listen, I've got to go – I've got a geography project to finish (OK, to *start*), and Peaches is nibbling my toes in a really annoying way. Just read this attachment – and I bet you two KitKats and a Mars Bar you'll be gobsmacked and reeling too. . .

Miss you ☹, but M8s 4eva ☺!
stella

PS And you really *are* my mate forever, Frankie, even if there were times during the holiday when it didn't seem like it at *all*. . .

Chapter 1

Signs of the sweet, sticky and furry kind. . .

"Bye, Stella!"

"Wave bye-bye to your sister, boys!"

"Phone us! Or text!"

"Yeah! Every day!"

"Don't forget!"

"BYEEEEEEE!!"

"Wuff!"

Good grief. You'd think I was *emigrating*, instead of just going away for a week's holiday.

Seven-and-a-half people and a dog – that's how many people (and dogs) had come to see me off at Portbay train station this morning.

The seven-and-a-half was made up of two adults (Mum and Dad), four teenagers (my friends TJ, Rachel, Amber and Tilda), and three kids (I counted my twin brothers as two halves, and TJ's little sis Ellie as another). Oh, and the dog was Bob – TJ's hairy Alsatian – who was barking at the train. (The train didn't seem too terrified.)

Watching them all from inside, from my seat by the window, what intense feeling swirled around my chest?

I'll tell you what feeling: guilt.

Guilt, guilt, guilt.

I was swamped in the stuff.

Mum was making me feel guilty, waving with both hands and struggling not to cry.

Dad was making me feel guilty, crouching down and trying to coax the twins into blowing me kisses (Jake was picking his nose and Jamie was trying to escape and chase pigeons instead).

My friends were making me feel guilty, holding up their corny-but-sweet homemade banner, struggling to keep it steady as a brisk October wind breezed in from the sea.

And the reason I felt swamped with guilt was that Mum and Dad and my mates were making such a big thing of saying goodbye, but all *I* could think of was the chorus of hellos I'd be hearing at the other end of this train journey.

Please let the whistle blow! I thought, fidgeting in my seat, longing to be on the move and get away from the guilt.

I waved through the window yet again, my grin

giving me face-ache, wondering if I could sneak a peek at my watch, or if that would look too obvious – not to mention heartless – to everyone who'd come to see me off.

It's not that I didn't love them, but I couldn't wait to be in London. It wasn't just 'cause I'd see Auntie V, or Frankie and my other mates, it was *especially* because of. . .

"Oof! Made it just in time!" said a woman, collapsing down on to a seat across the table from me, armed with a pile of magazines and a bulging, brightly-patterned shopper.

I smiled a weedy I-don't-want-to-be-rude, but-I-don't-really-want-to-get-stuck-in-a-conversation sort of smile in her direction. She looked nice, like a mumsy type mum (if you know what I mean), rather than a quite-groovy-for-a-mum type mum like mine. But still, it was nearly three hours to London, and I was dying to listen to the iPod my dad had let me borrow.

Pheeeeeeep!

At last – the whistle. And here we were, setting off with a hiccup of grinding mechanical somethings, as the train began to pull out of the station.

"Bye!" I mouthed at Mum and Dad and my little brothers.

"Bye!" Mum and Dad called back, as Jake and Jamie wriggled and squiggled.

"Bye!" I mouthed at TJ, Rachel, Amber and Tilda.

"Bye!" TJ, Rachel, Amber and Tilda shouted back, as TJ's dog Bob panted and his sister Ellie gleefully tap-danced.

Bye! I said silently to the sea, the endless blue sky and the soaring gulls. (I obviously didn't get a reply.)

"Quite a send-off you got there!" said the mumsy mum, while I was still waving, and before I got the chance to reach for my white iPod earphones.

"Mmm," I muttered, twisting round to catch a last glimpse of my own, personal crowd.

"So, I'm guessing your name is Stella, then?" the woman teased me gently.

No, she wasn't a mind-reader; she'd spotted it on the banner, same as absolutely everyone else on the train must've. ("SO LONG, STELLA!" was spray-painted on an unrolled length of wallpaper.)

"Mmm," I muttered again, smiling another weedy smile.

"Pleased to meet you, Stella. I'm Denise," said the mumsy mum, not particularly put off by my

6

non-committal "mmm's". "I recognize a few members of your fan club, there. . ."

"*Do* you?" I said in surprise, forgetting to be non-committal.

"Well, the boy and the little girl and the dog – I always see them down at the beach," said Mumsy Denise, starting to unpack stuff from her shopper. "You can't really miss a threesome like that, can you?"

"That's TJ, Ellie and Bob," I explained, without explaining that TJ was the short, funny boy and Bob was the big, dopey dog. (Ellie the five-year-old, tap-dancing cutie was pretty obvious.)

"And you can't miss Tilda Gilmore, can you?"

"You know her?" I asked, wondering what connection there could be between Mumsy Denise and Tilda, the tutu-and-leather-jacket-wearing town freak.

"Well, I'm *always* in and out of her dad's shop for bits and bobs."

Poor Tilda. For proper goth credentials, it would be better to have a father who'd been a roadie for Ozzy Osbourne, or the proprieter of a witchcraft museum or something, instead of a just a bloke behind a counter in a hardware store.

"And I know the tall girl . . . Amber, isn't it? Her mother cuts my hair," continued Mumsy Denise, snapping the tops off a couple of Tupperware plastic boxes. "And that dark-haired girl – her mum's gift shop is lovely when you're looking for a present!"

Of *course* this woman might know some of my friends; Portbay was the size of a wizened peanut compared to the gargantuan urban sprawl of London. Of *course* she might know my friend Amber, either from the Style Compony (Amber's Mum's misspelling), or from being served by Amber (badly, probably) during her weekend shifts at the Hot Pepper Jelly café. And of *course* Mumsy Denise would've noticed Rachel, who was easily one of the prettiest girls in town (though sadly, Rachel knew it).

"So, Stella," said Mumsy Denise, "going somewhere nice for the half-term holiday?"

"Home."

As soon as I said it, I jumped – which must have looked strange, like I'd sat on a drawing pin or something.

I hadn't *meant* to say home. Or had I? London had been home for the first thirteen years of my life, and Portbay had been home for about three-and-a-half months. So mathematically, did that still make London more of my home than Portbay?

"I mean London. I'm visiting my Aunt Vanessa, but I used to live there. Till we moved here at the start of the summer," I corrected myself.

"Really? That's not very long ago. It must have been very difficult to make such a big move."

I nodded. "It was a bit."

It was a *lot*, I meant. From the moment my parents told me they were selling up and moving to Portbay, I felt sick. Sick at the idea of leaving my great gang of girls in London, of having no mates, and nothing to do in some run-down, sleepy seaside resort.

"Did you make friends quickly?" asked Mumsy Denise, reaching into her bag for a fistful of serviettes.

"Sort of," I sort of answered.

I'd known Mumsy Denise for exactly one-and-a-half minutes, which didn't make me feel much like telling her stuff that would make her think I was *seriously* insane. Stuff like how my first friend in Portbay was a fat, scruffy cat who seemed to be psychic. (Though Peaches hadn't seemed very psychic today: all I saw was a flash of ginger tail as he bounced off the garden wall when I went in search of a goodbye cuddle.)

Or that the second friend I made was an eccentric old lady, who might or might not be a ghost. (Spookily, Mrs S-T did sound a lot like Tilda's ex-neighbour, who was a little bit, um, *dead*.)

Or that the third "friend" was a dilapidated house in a deserted cove. (There were no grand empty rooms to dance around in now – Joseph's House was gone and the developers were speeding on with the new holiday homes in Sugar Bay.)

Mind you, if Mumsy Denise *did* get the impression that I was seriously insane, maybe she wouldn't try talking to me for the next three hours. . .

"So what are you going to get up to in London?" my travel buddy suddenly asked, before I got the chance to faze her with my serious insane-ness. "Just catching up with old friends?"

OK, what I was planning on getting up to: that was something *else* I wasn't about to blurt out to someone I'd only known for . . . let me see, nearly two minutes now. I mean, you don't tell just *anyone* you're on a very secret mission.

Specially a very mad, impossible secret mission to find a person who's so much part of you and so much an almost nameless stranger. . .

"Uh, yeah, just catching up with old friends," I agreed, half-lying.

My stomach squidged nervously – not just 'cause of the half-lying, but because I suddenly wondered if I had the remotest chance of making my very mad, impossible secret mission work.

"Fairy cake?" asked Mumsy Denise, shaking a sweet-smelling plastic box under my nose.

Fairy cakes.

Cue another stomach-squidge.

Y'know, ever since I'd thought up my secret mission, I'd been looking for *some* kind of sign – some little clue or spooky coincidence that might give me an inkling that I was on the right track.

And now these fairy cakes . . . they might just be *it*.

Does that make sense?

Yeah, I know. As much sense as fish ice cream.

But it's like this: I'd never thought about signs and coincidences very much, till I moved to Portbay. And then they came thick and fast, till I practically relied on Peaches giving me one of his intense green-eyed cat stares, or bumping into cheery, odd Mrs S-T feeding fat, psycho seagulls with toffees and fairy cakes pulled from the depths of her teeny-tiny handbag. And with that certain cat stare or that sudden sighting of Mrs S-T, I'd know that something interesting or strange or maybe a little bit wonderful was just around the corner.

But I hadn't seen Mrs S-T in the flesh (or otherwise) since the end of the summer, since shortly after Joseph's House burned down. And lately Peaches had been more interested in his tuna kitty chunks than sending me any telepathic messages.

"Thank you!" I smiled warmly at Mumsy Denise, relaxing back in the seat with my fairy cake, my edible good luck charm.

And for the next hour or two, I relaxed more, letting Mumsy Denise feed me bits of her on-board picnic and tit-bits about her life. It was kind of nice in a numb way to hear about the sister she was going to visit, and the days out they were planning on having. The more I heard about garden centres and knitting exhibitions, the more I felt all the Portbay guilt slipping away, and the London excitement building. . .

"Ooh, I think we've eaten just about everything!" Mumsy Denise laughed, gathering up her collection of empty plastic tubs. "Still, I'm sure we've got room for a sweet!"

A bag of sticky toffees.

Time for yet another stomach-squidge.

Sticky Toffee was the nickname I gave Mrs S-T

in the first days that I knew her, before I found out that a) her real name was very possibly Mary Duggan, and b) she might be a ghost.

"Thank you," I said as calmly as I could, taking the sweet and unravelling the rustly paper.

Three seconds later, I wasn't so calm. Well, it's quite hard to be calm when you're choking to death on a toffee.

"Dear me!" gasped Mumsy Denise, quickly coming around to my side of the table and patting me on the back. "What happened there?"

What happened? I'd just bitten into the buttery sweetness when I'd idly glanced out at the tiny train station we were whizzing non-stop through.

We'd whizzed so fast that I couldn't make out the name of the station, or get a clear look at the faces of the passengers waiting for some slower commuter train to come by.

But I *still* managed to make out a curled ginger shape on the very last bench before the platform ran out.

I guess I shouldn't have tried to squawk out the name "Peaches!" with my teeth glued together with toffee. (I got as far as "P" before I started choking.)

"I'm OK," I finally managed to say, getting my

breath back, and hoping my face wasn't too embarrassingly, luminously red.

And I *was* OK. I mean, prize wanderer that he was, even Peaches couldn't have magically travelled a whole two hours' train ride away (could he?). But that green-eyed lookalike was good enough for me.

After all, they say things come in threes.

And those three sweet, sticky and furry signs suddenly made me feel pretty sure that my very mad, impossible secret mission might just (somehow, some way) be possible after all. . .

Chapter 2

The secret of the mad secret mission

Heaven.

When I got a minute, that's what I'd tap back to Tilda, who'd just texted me and asked what Auntie V's flat was like.

White walls, white carpets, cream sofas, vanilla cushions, bleached wood furniture. All that ethereal light and brightness would probably be Tilda's idea of hell, but I think God might feel right at home here, if he ever dropped in for a cup of tea. All that was missing was a cloud gently drifting by. (I'm pretty good at art – maybe I'd have to offer to paint a few on Auntie V's ceilings sometime. . .)

Don't know what God would make of Auntie V's antique theatre posters though (the only non-neutral things in her house); some of them were a bit dramatic, with crazed-looking Victorian women holding daggers or whatever. Still, I guess the Bible's got some bloodthirsty, gory bits in it too, so he might not mind. . .

Anyway, a three-hour train journey and a three-quarter-hour taxi ride later, and here I was in Auntie V's heavenly flat in pretty, posh Highgate. And I was feeling kind of *blah*.

From guilty, to wow! to *blah*, my moods had been taken on a real rollercoaster ride today. So what had happened in the last while to get me from wow! to *blah*?

Well, I'd come off the train at Paddington Station on a total high: high on excitement (my mad, secret mission was almost about to start), high on sugar (too many fairy cakes and toffees), and high on happiness (the thought of seeing Frankie and the girls again).

And then just as I was saying bye to Mumsy Denise, I spotted that the only person waiting to meet me was Auntie V. Gorgeous, elegant (sarky) Auntie V, smiling and waving my way.

What I'd *really* had in my head was a gaggle of screaming girlies, tearing down the platform towards me, bursting my eardrums with their squealing and my ribs with their hugs.

But it was stupid of me to expect them, really. I mean, I hadn't *asked* Frankie and everyone to come, and they hadn't offered. I just sort of *hoped* they might want to surprise me, that's all. But if I thought about it sensibly (and I did in the black cab home to Auntie V's), Kentish Town to Paddington is an hour's faffing about on buses and tubes.

And after all, the original plan was that I'd see them tomorrow, for a bit of a very special, old-skool treat.

"You're meeting the girls in Marine Ices?" said Auntie V, dropping a couple of extra fluffy white towels on the single bed in her spare room-cum-office. "Can't say that's one of my favourite restaurants!"

Well, there was a surprise, *not*.

Auntie V was as groomed and Nordically white as her flat. Hanging out in a cheesy fifties-style Italian café and ice-cream parlour didn't really fit with her look. (Pasta sauce and chocolate ice cream would be a total pain to get out of ivory linen trousers, I guess. . .)

"So, Stella, my little star," said Auntie V, fixing me with a smile as she gently wound her fingers around one of my tangle of curls. "As of tomorrow, Stella Etc. will be together again, just like the old days!"

Yep, the old days, when Auntie V couldn't be bothered to remember Frankie, Parminder, Lauren, Eleni and Neisha's names. The old days, when she came up with calling us Stella Etc. for short.

"Yep. It'll be great," I agreed, reminding myself

that it really *would* be. I mean, before I even got talking to my friends about my very mad, impossible secret mission, I had so much to show and tell. In my pink, pull-along suitcase I'd got a folder of stuff torn out of the local papers, featuring me and my (Portbay) mates.

Bleep!

Another text – from Frankie, maybe, to sort out a meet-up time for tomorrow.

"I'll leave you to get unpacked," Auntie V mouthed at me, retreating out of the room with a flick of her neat, white-blonde bob.

As soon as she was gone, I checked out the message on the screen of my mobile.

Wuff, wuff, wuff, wuff! Luv Bob x, it read.

Very funny, I thought, grinning at TJ's daft message.

Chucking the phone on the bed, I started unzipping my suitcase. I wasn't going to get back to TJ quite yet, or Tilda, for that matter – like Auntie V said, I should unpack first.

"And *this* is first. . ." I muttered out loud, used to having fat, friendly, weird Peaches around to talk to in my room at home.

"This" was a small plastic bag, pulled from the top of my stuffed case. Gently, I spilled the contents out. . .

- One soft plastic wallet, with an old paper library card in it (plus a surprise something else folded in the back)
- An old perfume bottle, empty, label missing
- A folding paper fan, decorated with birds of paradise
- A small hardbacked envelope

The plastic wallet, the perfume bottle and the fan had come from the cardboard box stuffed at the back of my parents' wardrobe – the one marked "Mum's things", written in my own mum's handwriting. Most of the stuff was made up of documents to do with my Nana Jones's life: house and life insurance, birth certificate and (sadly) death certificate. Only the plastic wallet (with the surprise tucked inside), the bottle and the fan felt like they meant something personal rather that legal.

And the hardbacked envelope. . . Well, I tipped it up now and let a black and white photo slip out into my hand. My one and only photo of my Nana Jones and Grandad Eddie together. I propped it up on the bedside table, against a white pottery lamp.

"Hello," I whispered to the two teenagers smiling out at me, the clutter of a fairground in the background behind them.

Auntie V had a beautiful, ornate silvered mirror by her desk, right above her laptop. I couldn't resist standing up and staring into it, glancing between my reflection and the photo, from the two very different faces from forty years ago that seemed to meld into . . . well, *me*. Grandad Eddie's tight black curls morphed into my honey-brown ringlets; Nana Jones's heart-shaped face and almond eyes were the double of mine, though you couldn't see our matching freckly noses, since Nana's were hidden under a layer of the heavy make-up that was fashionable back in the sixties.

You know, Auntie V's mirror looked like something out of a fairy tale, which is why Nana Jones and Grandad Eddie's story suddenly felt like it should begin with a once upon a time. How would it go?

Once upon a time, there was a girl who fell in love with a boy, who loved her right back. They were blissfully happy, till the girl's parents decided they didn't approve of the boy, and made their daughter give him up. Heartbroken, the boy left town, still loving the girl, who still loved him. . .

Still, that's not much like most fairy tales, where

the prince always marries the heroine in the end, despite cruel spells, wicked step-mothers and poisoned apples. This particular story was more of a tragedy, like *Romeo and Juliet* or something.

Only Romeo was my Grandad Eddie and Juliet was my Nana Jones. And the reason Nana Jones's parents didn't approve of him was because a) Grandad Eddie worked for a travelling fair, and b) he was black. But if my great-grandparents thought Eddie moving on with the fair was the end of their troubles, it wasn't. Grandma Jones was hiding a secret that she hadn't even told Eddie about. And that secret would turn out to be . . . my mum.

"It was 1965, remember," Mum said to me a couple of months ago, when we'd sat going through the box of Nana Jones's stuff. "Going out with someone who was a different colour, and having a baby without being married . . . well, it was just ignorance, but people thought of both those things as pretty shocking."

I flopped back down on the bed and gazed at those hopeful faces in the photo, trying to see if there were any doubts in their eyes: doubts that this bright, shiny bliss wasn't going to last.

Did they have the *slightest* clue that their story wasn't going to have a happy ending. . .?

"Hey –"

At the sound of Auntie V's voice approaching the bedroom door, I quickly sat on the bulk of the evidence (I hoped the fan wouldn't snap).

"– I thought we could take a walk along to Café Rouge for tea tonight for a special treat, yes?"

"Sure!" I said, convinced that I had guilt written all over my face, for the second time today.

I didn't want Auntie V to see Nana Jones's stuff and ask what it was. I didn't want her to end up phoning Mum and telling her I'd taken it without letting her know. And I definitely didn't want my very mad, impossible secret mission to come out. . .

"Good." Auntie V nodded. "Then I'd better just give the restaurant a call and make sure they're not booked up, since it's Saturday night."

"Right," I answered, trying to subtly move a butt-cheek so that my weight wasn't on the delicate fan any more.

"Fine," shrugged Auntie V, moving away and probably wondering why the conversation had turned so stilted.

As the door closed behind her, I quickly gathered up the special bits and pieces, dropped them back in the bag and zipped the whole thing into the side pocket of my case.

I was dying to re-read the letter – the one I'd found tucked into the back of the old plastic wallet – but I'd save that for later, once the flat was quiet and Auntie V was in bed.

But oops – I'd forgotten the photo.

Picking it up, I smiled back at the carefree couple.

"Grandad Eddie," I whispered, gazing into his deep, dark eyes, "I'm coming to find you."

And *that* was the secret of my very mad, impossible secret mission: trying to find a lost grandad.

Even though that might mean chasing a ghost. . .

Chapter 3

The girly get-together gone wrong. . .

Marine Ices: a fifteen-minutes stroll, or a ten-minute race (if we were in that kind of stupid mood), from Camden Lock Market.

All of our parents knew that *this* was where me and Frankie and the girls would want to be, if they felt like treating us.

For instance, at exam-time – we always came here when they finished.

And we came here for Frankie's thirteenth birthday, when she got us all giggling by insisting on standing on a chair and posing while we sang happy birthday to her.

We came here for Parminder's birthday too, when her big brothers Ajeet and Dhann embarrassed her by squidging their noses up against the plate glass window.

We came here after Eleni's gran died and she needed cheering up.

We came here after Lauren's mum and dad announced they were splitting up.

We came here when Neisha's mum and her mum's lovely boyfriend decided to get married.

We came here the week before I moved to Portbay. . .

"You couldn't finish your Coppa Gino ice-cream for crying! Remember, Stella?" said Lauren, reaching over the Formica table to touch my arm.

"I remember crying, but I don't remember eating a Coppa Gino!" I laughed at Lauren, who was, reassuringly, as dippy as ever. "I don't like almonds!"

"Yes, you do!" She frowned her fair eyebrows at me. "You *love* almonds!"

"No, she *doesn't*!" Parminder corrected her, reassuringly as teacher-like as ever.

"Well, who does, then?" Lauren frowned some more.

"*Seb*, you idiot!" Neisha laughed, slouching on the table and twirling a spoon in anticipation of the Chocolate Nut Cup that was coming her way any minute. "He *always* has that when we come here. . ."

Uh-oh.

Neisha had no sooner mentioned Seb's name than all the girls turned their heads to stare at me.

For the last twenty minutes it had been niggling me that Frankie still hadn't shown up yet (how keen was my best-est, oldest friend to see me exactly?), but now I was glad. Without making her (and me) feel awkward, I could say straight out what my mates seemed to find so incredibly hard to believe.

"Look, it's OK! Honestly! It's *so* long ago it doesn't matter, and me and Frankie are fine about it!"

Well, I hadn't exactly been fine when I found out that Frankie had started dating the boy I fancied, about five seconds after I left London. And I wasn't fine about arguing with her over it when she came to stay with me, a week after I moved to Portbay. But all that felt like forever ago now.

Neisha and Lauren, Eleni and Parminder . . . they all looked at me slightly pityingly, as if they didn't believe it for a second.

I felt bubbles of frustration rush in my chest. I wasn't shy little Stella any more: I wasn't the girl who used to let my friends do the ordering for me in here, just in case asking for a cassata (my favourite) started my stammer up. I wasn't poor little Stella who had a crush on a cool older boy who'd never think of her as girlfriend material, certainly not while loud, funny, gorgeous Frankie was kicking around Kentish Town. . .

Parminder (being Parminder) was the first to notice I might want the subject changed.

"Yeah, of course. So . . . what's your school like? Better than the rotten old Rochester?"

I shrugged. "It's kind of the same, and kind of not."

For a small town, Portbay had a big secondary school – bigger than the Rochester, even – 'cause kids came from towns, villages and farms all around.

The teachers were just like any other bunch of teachers; lots were nice, a few weren't, and the same went for the students. I guess the only difference was that practically everyone's skin colour was more or less whiter-than-white – not including mine, of course. Actually, there were more people from different ethnic backgrounds sitting round this table than there was in the whole of Portbay School (Neisha: black, Lauren: white, Parminder: Asian, Eleni: Greek, me: three-quarters white and one-quarter from Barbados).

"You said you'd bring photos – I'm *dying* to see what Tilda looks like!" said Neisha, perking up.

"Sure! I'll get them out."

I pulled out the folder of newspaper pages I'd

brought along with me; they were out of order after me and Auntie V had pored over them on her sofa late last night. (It was brilliant the way she'd been so interested, but I had been slightly stressed the whole time about getting black newspaper fingerprints on the cream sofa.)

"Here's a good one," I said, choosing the first interview we'd done for the local paper, where me and my Portbay mates were pointing to the amazing, vast chandelier in the ballroom of Joseph's House.

"Are you in *all* of these?" Neisha asked, thumbing through the fairly thick pile of newsprint.

"Not all of them," I explained, while Parminder, Lauren and Eleni noseyed at the one I'd passed across the table. "Some of them are about the campaign to save the chandelier before the house got demolished –"

Neisha blinked at me blankly, like I was reciting the seventy-five times tables at her.

"– some are about finding the gravestones of Joseph and Elize Grainger –"

I'd hoped Neisha might manage an interested "oh!", but long-dead black servant boys and plantation owner's daughters were obviously like very *dull* ancient history to her.

"– and there's some stuff about . . . um . . . just other stuff. It doesn't matter." I trailed off, stopping before Neisha went comatose on me and slipped under the table in a bored heap. The signs so far didn't exactly point to her being fascinated by the pets' graveyard we'd found in the grounds of Joseph's House, just before the fire tore through it.

"Hey, are there any pictures of your ghost lady?" Eleni asked, glancing wide-eyed at the pile of papers under my hand.

"Duh!" Parminder laughed at Eleni. "She's a *ghost*! Ghosts don't do cheesy smiles for local papers!"

Maybe I was suddenly feeling super-sensitive (the latest in my rollercoaster ride of moods), but was Parminder having a go at me, there? After all, she'd just been staring at my picture in the paper only a nano-second before. Was she saying *I* was smiling all cheesily?

"Look, like I said in my e-mails," I cut in, "I don't know if Mrs S-T really *is* a ghost. She didn't seem very ghostly all the times I met her."

Mad as a goat, but not remotely floaty like a ghost. I mean, I'd never heard of ghosts wearing marshmallow pink netted hats and apple-green raincoats.

"But you said your friend Tilda—"

"It might just be a coincidence. I'll probably bump into Mrs S-T next week, feeding the seagulls or something," I interrupted Eleni quickly. I was suddenly feeling protective of Mrs S-T, specially now that Neisha and Lauren were making Scooby-doo "whooOOOOoooooo!" noises.

"So where *is* Tilda?" asked Parminder, putting her head down and scouring the clipping of the ballroom again. "I really want to see this tutu. . ."

"Oh, she's not in that one. Neither's Amber. That was before I got to know them. There's just me, TJ, his little sister Ellie, the pretty girl is Rachel, and that's Megan."

"So are you still in touch with her, then?" asked Parminder, sitting back in her seat, having seen quite enough of the *Portbay Journal* after ten seconds' perusal. "That girl Megan, I mean?"

"Yeah – she texted me last night, actually."

I hadn't got back to Megan yet. But mentioning her made me feel a bit better. It's just that so far, my London girlfriends only seemed interested in the freak show side of what I had to tell them: Tilda's nuts outfits and the fact that my old lady friend might not be real. Yeah, I knew that stuff *was* kind of wow, but there was so much more I

30

wanted to share with them. Like how brilliant all my friends were, including Megan, who I'd met when her family were on holiday in Portbay.

"She's maybe coming to stay with me at New Year," I chatted on. "That would be brilliant – she's such a laugh. And—"

"Hold on," Neisha butted in. "Megan – she's the really loud, sort of dopey one who does cartwheels?"

"*Dippy*. I think I said in my e-mails that she was a bit *dippy*," I said defensively.

"You know, it's amazing," said Parminder, suddenly leaning towards me and studying me like a science experiment. "You'd have stammered really badly trying to say that before!"

These were my closest mates, and yet I was blushing and uncomfortable as they all turned to stare at me, like I was a worried frog in a tank in a biology lab.

"When did it go?" probed Lauren.

In my flustering, I hadn't a clue what she was on about. In fact, it took a couple of seconds of shaking *frogs* out of my head to realize that Lauren was talking about my stammer.

"I don't exactly know." I shrugged. "I've just been so busy in Portbay . . . and it just sort of wasn't there one day."

My friends were pleased for me, I tried to tell myself. But it wasn't much fun being reminded of a part of me that I didn't think of with a whole lot of fondness.

"YAAAAAAAAAYYYYYY, STELLLAAAAA!!"

At last – Frankie! Who cared if she was twenty minutes late! Now we could have a laugh, talk about stuff that wasn't my stammer, and even plan out some of my secret mission. Maybe after we'd finished eating I could take the treasured letter out of the back of Nana Jones's plastic wallet and show them. . .

Turning and screeching my chair back, I was ready to blast a grin Frankie's way, along with all the other girls.

But as I saw my best friend stride towards me, I froze, a ripple of ice shooting up my spine.

What was Frankie trying to do to me? Being late for me, for our special girls' get-together, I could deal with. But I wasn't sure I could deal with the extra "guest" Frankie had brought along with her.

There was no getting away from the hug I suddenly found myself squashed in, or the squeals of "Stella" directly in my ear. And there was no getting away from the fact that I was looking directly over Frankie's shoulder at her boyfriend.

I'd just have to try and be chilled-out about this, even if it was just to prove to Parminder and Neisha and the others that I was OK, I was fine.

"Hi, S-S-S-Seb," I heard myself stammer.

When exactly was the next train back to Portbay. . .?

Chapter 4

The lost and found stammer

A fictitious wee: that's what I was having.

Anything to buy me a little time on my own, to get away from . . . well, not so much Frankie and Seb, but Frankie and her amazing lack of sensitivity. Ten out of ten for stomping all over my feelings.

Didn't she have a *clue* just how plain *wrong* it was to bring her boyfriend – my ex-major crush – along today. . .?

Y'know, before I'd gone for my fictitious wee, I think quite possibly *everyone* – and I mean waiters, waitresses, people at neighbouring tables, and not just my mates – felt the awkwardness seeping from our corner of the restaurant. Well, all except Frankie, who held court, telling tales about the laugh she and Seb had just had at Ally Pally ice rink, and all about the hip-hop band he was trying to get together at school.

The girls chipped in with a whole slew of stories too, just to avoid cringey silences, I think. Parminder moaned about her new neighbours listening to a blaring ragga pirate radio station with their windows open all night; Neisha talked about her stepdad's bad habit of sleep-singing (at least it was Motown classics, which was better than ragga pirate radio stations); Eleni yakked on about her cousin Georgiou crashing his new scooter into a bollard while he was yelling "Hello, baby!" at a cute girl on Camden High Street, and Lauren showed me her belly-button piercing that *still* hadn't healed properly (yewww).

Only me and Seb said nothing much: Seb, because Frankie was doing all the talking for him, and me because I didn't fancy opening my mouth and letting yet another surprise stammer slip out.

It felt strangely lonely in the middle of my old gang all of a sudden, that was for sure.

Bleep!

I sat on the loo, having my fictitious wee, and stared at the message Amber had just texted me.

Having a good time? Hope so!

Tall, skinny, awkward Amber, whose hair matched her name but clashed horribly with her face when she was blushing (which was a lot of the time). She was probably doing a holiday shift in the Hot Pepper Jelly café right now, taking a break from serving Coke and muffins to TJ and Rachel, or muddling up the orders for a bunch of holidaymakers (as usual).

Y'know, growing up in London, I'd considered myself to be the reigning Queen of Shyness. Then I moved to Portbay and met Amber, and realized I was merely a Princess of Shyness, or maybe even just a distant cousin of the Duchess of Shyness.

She'd really feel for me now, hiding in a toilet cubicle in a faraway café, wishing a rip in the fabric of the universe would happen in this very loo, so that I could slip into it and never have to slouch my way back to the table outside ever again.

"Stella? You in here, Stel?"

Parminder. She, out of everyone, would've clocked how long I'd been gone for.

"Yeah, coming," I said, flushing the toilet quickly for effect.

I pulled open the door to see her concerned face looking into mine.

"Just texting one of my friends," I said hastily.

"Oh," she murmured, as I squeezed past her and hurried back into the main room of the café.

I didn't want to get caught up in a discussion with Parminder about whether I was "OK" – translation: "You really, truly *do* still have a thing for Seb, don't you, Stella, huh?"

The thing was, I really, truly *didn't* have a thing for Seb. I just had a thing about supposed best mates assuming you don't have any feelings. Since Frankie (and Seb) had arrived, Frankie had asked me if my brother Jamie was still biting people (he was) and if TJ had grown any more or if he was still as big as a dormouse (just about), and that was it. She'd seemed more interested in talking to, at or about Seb. My folder of newspaper features lay ignored on the table, till a waitress shoved it over to make room for the ice creams.

The plastic wallet – and the secret love letter tucked in the back – stayed unseen and unshared in my bag. . .

"Hey, Stella!" Frankie yelled out as I slunk into my chair, banging her hands on the table and making the empty dishes and sticky spoons rattle.

"Leave it out, Frankie!" said Seb, grinning as he pulled her close and jokily slapped his hands across her mouth.

Oh, no. What had she been saying to him? What total humiliation was coming *next*?

Frankie wasn't about to be shut up, and easily

freed herself from Seb's attempts to gag her.

"I was just saying that you should draw Seb!!"

Seb. If I'd wanted to do it, he'd have been brilliant to draw – tall, slim face and long nose (from his Somali dad), floppy mid-brown hair (from his Brummie mum) and a cute lopsided grin (all his own).

But that was the thing: I didn't want to do it.

And Seb wasn't keen on me doing it either, from the way he'd been trying to shut Frankie up.

"I'm n-n-not really into caricatures any more," I mumbled.

Neisha, Lauren and Eleni were all staring at me. (That staring business was *definitely* starting to get to me.)

Maybe it was because they were stunned to hear I'd given up on the one thing I was kind of famous for at my old school. But somehow I found caricatures just too harsh now, and sometimes almost a bit cruel. In my den back in Portbay, I had my most recent invention – my Ninja fairies – pinned along the edge of the shelves. They were what I found myself doodling again and again. But I didn't suppose über-cool Seb, with his hip-hop credentials, would be too impressed by some dumb manga fairies. . .

"I c-c-can't, Frankie," I protested. "I haven't got

anything to draw with."

Neisha, Lauren and Eleni stared some more. Was it because they couldn't believe I'd lost and found my stammer so quickly?

I didn't dare look at Seb to see what *he* made of my stammer.

"Here! Use this!" Frankie spread a red paper napkin out in front of me, and pulled a black pen out of her bag for me to use. "Wait till you see *this*, Seb – Stella does the most amazing caricatures! They're so good they could go up on the wall here!"

Frankie pointed to the signed photos of celebs who'd come into the café over the years (and who presumably loved ice cream). A crummy caricature of mine wasn't *ever* going to be framed and hung here.

"I r-r-really can't—"

Bleep!

Hi . . . 4gotten us? . . . love. . .

Without taking time to properly read what the incoming text said, I immediately skimmed down and saw it was from Rachel.

"It's from my Auntie V," I fibbed out loud. "She wants to pick me up earlier than we agreed. I've got to go."

Maybe they knew I was lying. Parminder and

Frankie, I mean, and maybe Eleni too, since they were the sharpest of my friends (sorry Lauren, sorry Neish).

If any of them could read my mind, they'd know that Auntie V wasn't so much waiting for me, as spending the afternoon in 1967, watching a DVD of some hippy-era musical that she loved, called *Sweet Charity*.

Quickly grabbing my folder and shoving it into my canvas bag, I mumbled "Bye" to everyone, and turned to go. Behind me came a chorus of "See you tomorrow!"s (not from Seb, thankfully), so maybe my friends *had* remembered the plan we'd made by e-mail these last couple of weeks.

Getting ready to pull on the handle of the glass entrance door, I was *just* about to escape Marine Ices with my dignity intact – even if my mood was scraping the ground – when Frankie called out to me.

"Hey, Stella!"

"Uh-huh?" I said, turning around.

"Don't know what it's like in the country, but don't you guys ever pay for stuff?" she grinned, pointing to the cassata that I'd hardly touched.

Urgh. I'd forgotten to leave any money.

Trudging back to the table like a naughty five-year-old, I clumsily pulled a few pound coins out of my pocket and plonked them there, feeling my face flush as raspberry red as Amber's in her worst omigod moment.

Then gathering myself together, I turned to leave again, but tripped straight over a bag tangled around the nearest chair.

"Comfy enough for you?!"

That was Seb, as I fell backwards and landed in his lap.

Arrrgh. . .

Shoving the heel of my hand into his shoulder (it must have hurt) I sharply pushed myself up again, and for the second time, headed for the door.

"P-P-Peaches. . ." I whispered as I walked past the ice-cream counter on the way out, thinking of my ridiculously scruffy cat's ridiculous habit of smelling of peaches 'n' cream. "*Please* help me get out of here without looking like a total moron!"

At that second a waiter came waltzing behind me with a cake lit with a whole heap of candles. And a whole heap of people began singing "Happy Birthday" at the top of their voices, which immediately made everyone in the café turn their heads to see who the birthday boy or girl was.

"Thank you!" I sighed out loud, as I slipped anonymously into the chilly afternoon air of

Camden.

And immediately tripped over a guy busking with tabla drums on the pavement right outside.

For the first time in my life, I might have been tempted to swear – if I hadn't worried about it coming out as a stammered fumbling mumble. . .

Chapter 5

And then there was Evie

Who'd've guessed that me and Auntie V could ever be such buddies? Growing up, I'd've reckoned there was as much chance of that as me losing my pet stammer.

Zoom back to the beginning of the year, and this is how we were, how it had always been: shy little me, intimidated by my super-confident, super-chic aunt with the fine line in sarcasm (I never knew what to say to her, and whatever I *did* say to her came out flat and dumb, with an extra sprinkling of stammering).

And then something finally went "click" with us. That something was my parents' plan to move to Portbay, which at the time, my aunt and I both thought of as quite possibly the worst idea in the history of really, really terrible ideas. And her fearlessly saying so to my mum and dad instantly made her my hero, instantly gave us stuff to talk (OK, moan) about together.

Auntie V might still be slightly confused about me doing a U-turn over the summer and coming to love my new home town, but somehow we'd never gone back to the awkward, out-of-step relationship we used to have.

"So is everything all right? You were a bit quiet this evening," asked Auntie V, as she appeared at my bedroom door, and struck a pose in her white silk pyjamas, with one hand resting on the door frame.

"Hey, you look like you're ready to burst into song!" I teased her brightly instead of answering her question.

It was Sunday night, and Auntie V had surprised me earlier – when I got back from Camden – by suggesting we had a girly night in together. She'd insisted we change into our pyjamas (hers elegant, mine scruffy) at seven o'clock, order in Japanese food and settle down to watch a double bill of her favourite films.

It was a nice thought, even though I'm not very keen on sushi, and the films weren't the sunny delight you might expect from musicals (being about murders – *Chicago*; and wars – *Cabaret*). But it was still pretty cool to be hanging out with Auntie V like that.

And even with raw fish, murders and war, it

was *much* more fun and chilled out than the tense girly get-together I'd had this afternoon. The girly afternoon that I hadn't wanted to talk to Auntie V about, just in case it got me wound up and started me tripping up on my words again.

"Well, *I* don't know! Here I am, come to say a polite goodnight to my favourite niece, and all I get is cheek!" Auntie V replied to my teasing, smiling wryly and arching an eyebrow at me.

"I'm your *only* niece!" I pointed out, settling in under the softest duvet ever. "And I wasn't being cheeky – you look as if you could easily star in either of those films tonight."

Auntie V threw back her head and laughed, instantly looking an awful lot like foxy Roxie Hart from *Chicago*.

"Stella, my little star – if I burst into song, all the dogs in the neighbourhood would start howling. And *please* stop me if I ever look like I'm going to do a high-kick – I'd probably break everything on the nearest shelf and do myself an injury."

Auntie V has a very cool job; she's an agent for actors who star in musical theatre. It's an odd kind of job to get into, but she did it 'cause she couldn't get the job she *really* wanted, which was being an actor who starred in musical theatre. The thing was, Auntie V might have looked fantastic, but to quote what Dad once said, when it came to dancing she had all the grace of a three-legged, bad-tempered warthog and a voice to match.

"OK. So I'll strap you to the nearest chair if I see your toes tapping or hear you humming, then," I joked back.

You'd never catch my dad in white silk PJs and a neat bobbed haircut, but the way she smiled back at me just now, Auntie V reminded me so much of him. Both tall, both Nordic-looking – even though they were born and brought up in Norfolk, where Granny and Grandad Stansfield still lived.

"By the way, that was a short phone call home tonight," said Auntie V, as if she was reading my mind.

"Mum said she had to rush and get some stuff done on the computer for tomorrow morning, and the boys were playing up with Dad and not going to bed."

I'd been pleased Mum had got some work (since giving up their cushy jobs at a magazine company in London, my parents were both pouncing on any freelance jobs coming their way, in between trying to renovate our crumbly cottage).

Also, I'd been pleased my parents couldn't talk for long tonight, since it stopped them asking me what my plans were for tomorrow (setting off on the trail of Grandad Eddie).

"Never mind – you can catch up with them tomorrow and find out what new DIY disasters your dad's had or what Animal and Gonzo have managed to break in your absence."

Mum, Dad, Jake (Animal) and Jamie (Gonzo) ... they suddenly felt so oddly, uncomfortably far away.

"By the way," Auntie V added, "when you next see Frankie, tell her that I'm going to treat the two of you to something very special on Friday evening, since that'll be your last night together."

"Are you?" I said in surprise, forgetting for a second that I was well miffed with my supposed best friend. "What is it?"

"Something I've been trying to fix up for a while, and I've just this minute found out that it's sorted," Auntie V said, speaking in riddles as she held up a chic mobile that she'd had hidden behind her back.

That reminded me; altogether today I'd had two texts from Amber (custom must be slow in the café), one each from TJ, Rachel, Tilda and Megan – not to mention another woofy one from Bob the dog (yeah, right!). I'd have to get back to them all tomorrow, or whenever I had time. . .

"But what's happening on Friday?" I asked Auntie V.

"Uh-uh. Not telling. Got to wait and see."

Arrrgh. How exciting, but infuriating not to know.

Sensing I was just about to push for more info, Auntie V reached across to her desk and scooped up her laptop, put a hand on the white porcelain doorknob and started pulling the door closed, with a soft *shhhhhhh* of cream pile carpet.

"Don't go!"

"Got to," Auntie V said briskly, escaping before I pestered her for more clues. "Got a few e-mails to do for work tomorrow. And you'll need your sleep, since you've got a busy day ahead, lounging around with your friends at Frankie's house!"

She blew a kiss and I blew her one back, before she shut the door, leaving me in the small-but-beautifully-formed room.

Little did she know there wouldn't be any lounging tomorrow. Me and Frankie and the girls would all be making our way over to Hackney in East London, on a bus route or three that I hadn't quite sussed out yet. That's if Frankie didn't bail out and go on a date with Seb instead. . .

Curled up in the small, cosy room, in a pool of warm white light that was radiating from the bedside lamp, I felt another ripple of loneliness. But then at least being alone meant I got a chance to take a long look at the letter again.

First, I took out the photo of the lovestruck teenagers and propped it up by the lamp, just to try and magic them in the room as I read. And then gently, gently I unfolded the fragile, softened, pale blue envelope. The address read *Evie Jones, 12 Cleveland House, Sewardstone Road, Hackney, London*. There was no stamp on it – it must have been hand-delivered.

Evie. . . began the letter inside, in dark blue ink handwriting.

Weird.

Weird to think of Nana Jones as Evie. Weirder somehow than the idea of Granny and Grandad Stansfield being Graham and Lucy. Maybe it was because they were alive, and she wasn't. I hadn't even had the chance to call her Nana Jones to her face, since she died before she was born.

Evie. . . I started to read again.

I told the blokes at the fair that I'd changed my

mind about quitting, and so we're packing up tonight and heading north.

Don't know how long I can stand it, though – even tonight, I kept thinking I saw your face in the mirror tiles as the waltzer cars whirled round. And I can't stand seeing girls in the crowd, wafting those cheap paper fans, like the one I let you win on my stall, the first night we met.

You know, I had a nightmare last night; I dreamt that I smelled your perfume again, and it killed me when I turned around and saw it wasn't you who was wearing it.

God, Evie. . . I didn't know Friday was the last time I'd see you, not till I read your letter! I can't believe your mum and dad pretended you weren't home those times I came round. . .

Most of all, I just can't believe this is it! I must have got it all wrong, but I kind of thought you and me might mean forever.

But maybe there's forever and ever, and maybe there's just Evie.

A special time, a special person, and I can't go back there, however much I want to.
Love you so much,
Eddie xxx

Eddie. That's as much of his name as I knew. Back in the summer of 1965, he'd worked on a fair in East London, where he met my Nana – well, Evie – and he left town when she told him it was over.

I guess you could say my very mad, impossible secret mission was like the whole needle-in-a-haystack thing, on a *ginormous* scale. Eddie wasn't necessarily in London, for a start. He wasn't necessarily in Britain, either; Mum pointed out that although he was just a little boy when his parents had emigrated from Barbados in the 50s, he might have thought about settling back there.

I flopped my head into the soft pillow and sighed, already feeling worn out by the wild goose chase I hadn't even started. I could've done with the guiding paw of Peaches right now, but he was miles away, probably snoozing on my bed, shedding a cat-shaped halo of ginger hairs all over it.

Blinking slowly, my eyes settled on the theatre poster on the wall, one of the more darkly dramatic ones in the flat. Médée, it said along the top, as a mad, starey-eyed woman held a dagger above some poor whoever at her feet. Cheery stuff (not).

And then I noticed something I'd never spotted before in this poster, this poster that I'd looked at plenty of times before, whenever I'd visited Auntie V's flat. Two feline green eyes, peering from the swathes of robes by the heroine's feet. . .

"Cool!" I could imagine Tilda saying at the sight of it. "Freaky!" I could imagine Lauren shuddering.

But those eyes in that gloomy poster; they made me feel strangely at home.

"Who needs a teddy bear when I've got a lookalike Peaches?" I whispered to myself and the green cat eyes.

Call it another sign (or call it crazy), but I felt I could sleep happy now.

Folding the note up and slipping it under the photo, I flicked the lamp off.

Bleep!

The green light on my mobile display interrupted my mad meanderings.

Soz so late – just texting 2 say I told girls not to come 2morrow. That OK? Just b good 2 b u & me. . . luv Frankie

Wow. . . Thank goodness she'd realized that she'd got it badly wrong by bringing Seb today. Thank goodness we had a chance to start again.

Yay, I thought happily, as I lay back in the bed and texted "That's great" to my friend in the dark. *Tomorrow's going to be brilliant, I just know. . .*

Pressing "send", I could already feel myself slipping into sleep, into dreams of fairgrounds and raw fish, dancing molls and heartbroken lovers, good friends and neon green eyes. . .

Chapter 6

Two aunties, two fibs

"Dooooooo, do-be-dooo-woooo!!"

Ah, a song from the legendary Frank Sinatra . . . being mangled by a skinny, middle-aged, bald bloke in a vest, hanging out of his first floor living room window.

Luckily, he didn't see me; when Clive was in the middle of his Sinatra repertoire he was so lost in the moment that his eyes were blissfully shut. Unlike his mouth.

I grinned up at him from the semi-shelter of a small leafy tree, pleased to see that some things hadn't changed since we moved out of the street.

And what about the people who'd bought our flat – the mum, the dad, the little girl and the grumpy ten-year-old boy in a football shirt that I remembered from a couple of viewings? Did they regret buying a place beside a one-man karaoke show? Or did they find it quite funny, like me and Mum and Dad did? (At least Mum and Dad did till the twins were born, and Clive's singing woke them from their baby snoozles.)

And what about our old place? Had the new owners repainted the pinky-fawn walls in the living room, the colour Mum had always loved and Dad had always hated? How long had it taken them to figure out that the flashy stainless steel shower *looked* good, but was actually deeply evil and liked spouting out boiling water when you least expected it? And had the little girl in the family found the tiny "hello!" I'd scratched into the paint on the back of the bedroom door?

I took a step sideways, and glanced up at my old bedroom window. The little girl might have chosen a white net panel with a star pattern on it, same as I had. Or lilac curtains, just like my old ones – little girls always liked pink or lilac (except for Tilda – she probably had black curtains with spiders on them when she was in nursery).

But my heart went "doof", as soon as I saw what I saw. The curtains were red, and rumpled, with a sort of . . . of *cannon* print on them. Ah, wait a minute . . . Arsenal, the football team. Which meant the *boy* had taken my old room!

I hadn't expected that. And I hadn't expected to feel so wobbly about it. Our flat, the look of my old room . . . this place really, really wasn't home any more.

As I stood there, not sure whether I was feeling wobbly and weepy, or just wobbly and weird, my stomach crunched in a knot as a familiar scent drifted and swirled on the breeze.

It was the sort of scent that you shouldn't smell in London, a city forty kilometres from the nearest stretch of coastline.

The scent of the sea.

Salty, seaweedy, ozone fresh, instantly triggering a tug of homesickness for Portbay and everyone there.

How bizarre to feel homesick for an old home and a new home at the same time.

I needed tea, biscuits and Frankie – this was all getting too surreal. . .

I was lost. Lost in the vast bosom and arms of Aunt Esme.

"My baby! My sweetheart! My Stella!"

Aunt Esme is as small and round as Auntie V is tall and thin. She's as black as Auntie V is white. Most of the time when I was growing up, she was as much of a mum to me as, well, Mum.

And that's Aunt Esme in a nutshell (though you'd need a very big nutshell to fit Aunt Esme in).

"You're so grown-up!" she gasped, letting me out of her hug so she could look at me. "You're so beautiful! I can't believe this gorgeous young woman in front of me is the same little baby girl I used to change messy nappies for!"

"Mum! Do you *have* to talk about 'messy nappies'?! You're embarrassing Stella!" groaned Frankie.

"Francesca – does this look like an embarrassed face?" asked Aunt Esme, cupping my chin and cheeks on both her hands and grinning broadly at me, a twinkle of a tear or two in her eyes.

It was true, Aunt Esme could never embarrass me – she just made me smile. And her booming laugh, comfy lap and wraparound arms made her the best childminder a girl could have had, whether I was tiny or a teenager.

"Mum, you're acting like it's been years since you last saw Stella, but it was only about three months ago that she left!" Frankie sighed, her fists on her bare hips, her pink tracksuit bottoms worn dangerously low-slung.

"Three months can feel like for ever, though, can't it, Stella, my love?"

"Mmm, yesh it can," I tried to reply, my face still squashed in Aunt Esme's hands.

"And your beautiful mum? How is she? And those *gorgeous* little boys. . ."

"'Gorgeous'? Mum – have you forgotten what Jake and Jamie are *like*?" said Frankie incredulously. "They're not *gorgeous* – they're lethal!"

They *were* a bit lethal. Last week alone I caught Jamie playing doggies with Jake and nearly strangling him with a skipping rope round his neck for a lead. And five minutes after being set free, Mum caught Jake on a chair in the kitchen, playing with the knobs on the gas cooker. (Luckily for Jake, the gas board had temporarily cut off our supply, till a repairman could fix the gas pipe Dad had just drilled a hole through.)

"Ah, they're just babies. They're cute!" announced Aunt Esme, letting go of my face with one of her hands and flapping it in the air, to wave away Frankie's negativity.

"Cute as baby alligators!" mumbled Frankie in my direction, rolling her eyes. "Mum – can we at least let Stella in the door?"

"Francesca, Francesca – my girl is always in such a rush!" sighed Aunt Esme, showing no signs of either dropping her remaining hand from my face, or moving off the doorstep. "How did that old juice ad on TV go? 'You got to chill with the still. . .'"

Frankie pulled an I-want-to-kill-her face behind her mother's back. And then an idea seemed to light up her huge brown eyes.

"Mum! Can I smell something burning?"

"Oh, my Lord!" gasped Aunt Esme, turning and scurrying off to the kitchen. "I was frying you girls some banana fritters for your picnic!"

"Picnic?" I mouthed at Frankie.

Frankie grabbed me into the best-friend hug I should have had yesterday and held me tight. I knew (from previous experience) that I probably wouldn't get a sorry out of her, but this hug felt like a near-enough-sorry to me. And the fact that Frankie had blown out the others so it was just me and her today said more than a simple sorry could anyway. I couldn't wait to tell her about Auntie V and the who-knows-what-treat on Friday night. . .

"I thought it was easier to tell her we were going up Hampstead Heath for a picnic," Frankie whispered in my ear, as she rocked me back and forth.

"I told Auntie V that I was just hanging out here today," I said, rocking my best friend back.

Two aunties, two fibs.

But it had to be done; neither of them would have been wild about a pair of thirteen-year-olds trekking off to a part of London they didn't know very well. Which was one of the reasons the mad, very secret mission was secret.

The other reason was—

"Hey!" said a voice behind me, from somewhere out on the landing.

My heart sank like a plummeting lift in a shaft. Not just at the sound of the familiar voice, but the speed at which Frankie's arms left me, as she threw herself at Seb.

"Yay! Hey, babes!"

"Just as well it was a *girl* I caught you hugging," I heard Seb tease her, his voice sounding muffled in her hug, "or you'd be in *real* trouble, Frankie!"

Before I turned and had to inevitably force a smile on my face, I saw Aunt Esme down the hall, peeking out of the kitchen to see what was up, tea towel in hand. In that second she raised her eyebrows at me, as if to say "Hmmm. . .".

I guess maybe it was a comfort to know that someone *else* wasn't convinced that a new boyfriend/old crush was the right kind of company when old friends were trying to spend time together.

"Seb's football game got cancelled today," said Frankie, as I turned around to see her draped over the boy with the lopsided grin. "So I told him he could come along to our, er, picnic!"

Frankie threw me a wink and a grin, as if Seb sharing our secret was the most fun thing ever.

I think I'd had more fun the time I tripped in my new flip-flops and tore half my toenail off. . .

Chapter 7

True love is bad for you

I didn't know how long I'd been staring at the building in front of me.

And I didn't know how long I'd *keep* staring at it.

Till the goosebumps faded away, I supposed.

"Wow!" murmured Frankie beside me. "That is . . . *awesome*. Better than the Taj Mahal!"

Then she dissolved into a fit of giggles, hitting my arm as if she'd made the best joke ever.

Yeah, so Cleveland House wasn't going to win any awards for architecture, and it wasn't going to become a listed building any time soon, I didn't suppose.

But this low, long, sandy-coloured block of 1950s flats was really important in the history of Evie. According to what Mum had told me over the years, Evie had only lived in four places:

1) Some place in Dalston, near Hackney, where

she was born, which had since been demolished.

2) A flat by Victoria Park in Hackney, where she and her parents had lived through most of her childhood, till she was seventeen.

3) A house in Walthamstow, North London, where her family moved, because of the "shame".

4) A flat in Hackney with her new baby Louise (my mum), which she lived in till she died, back in 1993.

There was no point in looking for the Dalston house, since it didn't exist any more. And anyway, that wasn't as important as this place, the place Evie was living at the time she met Eddie.

When Evie was the same age as me, I wondered, did she stand on one of those balconies, leaning on the railing, gazing at the greenery of the park, and wondering when her life would begin? (Little did she know it would begin in a flurry of fairground lights four years later, and stall soon after.)

Maybe her bedroom was at the back of the block, overlooking the canal – with its swans, ducks and flower-festooned houseboats – that separated the flats from the park itself.

I was lost in imagining her: a girl like me, only with fair hair in a bouffant style and wearing polo necks and ski-pants. A girl with freckles on her nose that she was glad to hide when she was old enough to wear make-up. A girl with a heart-shaped face and a soon-to-be broken heart.

"Now *that* I like!"

I wondered what had caught Frankie's attention, and saw that she was already slinking off in the direction of an ice-cream van that had just pulled up outside the gate – one of ten or twelve ornate entrances – into this vast, sprawling park.

"Want one, guys?" she called over her shoulder, making her tiny, tight dark plaits spin around.

"No, I'm OK," I said, shaking my head.

Frankie had a whole chunk of midriff on display. The thought of that much bare skin, the chill on the breeze and a huge Magnum White gave me a serious case of the shivers.

"Nah, nothing for me either," Seb called after her, walking towards me from the front entrance of the building. I hadn't even noticed him going over there.

"Sure, babes?" Frankie called out to him, walking backwards.

"Totally," he called, before turning to me like he was about to speak.

"Just a Coke or something, Seb?" Frankie persisted.

"No."

"Er, could do with a no *thanks*, Frankie!" Frankie teased her boyfriend.

"Whatever." He grinned, waving her away like an annoying fly.

I noticed Frankie's smile slip as she spun round on her new Reeboks.

"It was number twelve, right?"

I looked up and saw that Seb was glancing down at the envelope I was clutching in my hands.

"Um, yes."

"Well, the way the buzzer system on the door looks, I reckon it's that flat there, with the red flowers in the window boxes. Want to press the buzzer and speak to whoever lives there now?"

"N-no!" I spluttered, every nerve ending jangling with sudden shyness. I mean, what if an old lady lived there, and thought I was some teenage mugger? What if it was a big bloke with a pit bull, who started to swear at me through the intercom? What if it was a Kurdish family who couldn't speak any English and babbled at me in confusion?

No – it was enough that I had an actual balcony to focus on, thanks to Seb.

"Just *this*," I said, nodding at the flats in front of me, "this is great. Honest."

"No worries." Seb shrugged his angular shoulders.

The mood rollercoaster I'd been on since I'd arrived in London yesterday had thrown me high and low and round the loop-de-loop again today. I'd felt awash with nostalgia outside my old flat first thing this morning, awash with love for my oldest friend when Frankie was doing the rock-a-hug with me on her doorstep, and awash with resentment when Seb had turned up and become three's a crowd earlier on.

And now I was awash with . . . gratitude.

Well, what can I say? It was really kind of Seb to help work out which flat had been Evie's. And it had been kind of him to engineer it so that I sat with Frankie on the busy overland train on the way over from Camden Road Station to Homerton. It had also been kind of him to ask questions about my secret mission when we walked to Victoria Park, and ambled round it vaguely, looking for . . . I didn't know what exactly.

The gratitude thing didn't stop there. I'd appreciated the fact that Seb had suggested we give up on the park itself, and look for Evie's old home, and I'd appreciated it even more when he snuck into a newsagent at the edge of the park and took a peek in a copy of an A-Z to find out where exactly Sewardstone Road was (two minutes' walk from where we were, as it happened).

It was better than Frankie's contribution, which was to fool around and take the mick ("Parks are boring, unless you're a toddler or a hundred and ten. Who cares about tea and cake and paddling pools? If *I* was prime minister, I'd make it law that every park had a McDonald's and arcade games in it!"). And if she wasn't doing that, she was moaning continuously about her new trainers giving her blisters.

I hadn't told her yet about Auntie V's surprise treat on Friday night. Whatever it was, I wasn't sure if I felt like Frankie deserved it. . .

"So, how come you never checked this place out before?" asked Seb, nodding in the direction of the flats. "Didn't you say your mum was brought up in Hackney? Didn't she ever show you round here?"

"She lived at the other side of Hackney – near Hackney Central station," I said, remembering a couple of outings we'd had to kiddy shows at the Hackney Empire when I was little. On those trips, Mum had inevitably parked the car in a quiet backstreet just round the corner from the theatre. A quiet backstreet called Eleanor Road, the place where she and Evie had lived together in the top-floor flat in a Victorian terrace.

"Yeah, but wouldn't she have hung out here, with her mates?"

"But this wouldn't have been her local park – she was right beside London Fields," I explained.

Seb nodded, and stared up, like me, at the balcony of 12 Cleveland House.

"So one thing I don't get," Seb said, after a silent few seconds.

"Uh-huh?"

"How come you're keeping all this. . ." he paused for a second, trying to find the right words, "searching thing from your mum? Wouldn't she be into it?"

Ah. The two reasons for the secret mission being secret, Part 2.

I half opened my mouth, but nothing came out at first. Did I *want* to explain private, emotional stuff to this boy I hardly knew? All the time I'd liked him, I'd never talked to him more than a timid, mousy "hi". Nothing more than that till the night of my Leaving London party, when he'd amazingly, unbelievably shown up. Actually, he'd only come 'cause Frankie asked him; Frankie had only asked him as a special treat for me, but neither of us had the faintest clue that Seb had said yes 'cause he had a thing for *Frankie*. . .

I bit my lip. I didn't want to look at him; the idea of my eyes meeting his suddenly felt pretty private and emotional too.

And then I dived in. Private and emotional or not, none of my other friends seemed so interested in my secret mission. Especially Frankie, who I could now hear arguing with the ice-cream van guy about the size of her Flake.

"It's just . . . I always thought my mum had got over my nana dying," I began, looking at the block of flats rather than Seb. "I thought—"

"Seb! SEB!!" Frankie suddenly yelled out.

"What?" Seb answered, swivelling round to glance at her and sounding properly tetchy.

I guess he felt bad about Frankie interrupting, just when I was talking about something that wasn't so easy to talk about.

"Can you come here a second? Tell this guy he's ripping me off!" Frankie ordered, pointing at her Flake.

"Tell him yourself!" Seb frowned her way, then turned back to me. "Sorry. Go on, Stella."

"Well, um," I started to reply, feeling a bit thrown, "well, I thought my mum was all, y'know, 'life goes on' sort of thing. But then we looked at this box of my nana's stuff a couple of times, and both times, my mum got really upset."

He kissed me at my leaving party, I remembered, my brain unexpectedly dredging up the memory while I talked.

Just on the cheek. And he'd told me I was cute too, I remembered some more.

Urgh . . . Seb would be wondering why I'd turned into the Blush Queen.

"I guess it's 'cause thinking about a person who died is one thing," said Seb, thankfully looking back at the flats instead of at pink-faced me. "But looking at their stuff is maybe different, or harder, 'cause then it makes it more real."

Get back to thinking about Mum and Evie, I ordered myself sternly.

"Yeah. . . The second time it happened, I spoke to my dad afterwards, and he said that Mum hadn't been able to go near the box since she'd sorted Nana's things out after the funeral."

Seb didn't say anything else, which was fine. It was enough to know he understood.

70

"Anyway, so that's why she doesn't know what I'm doing now. And why I haven't shown her this yet. . ."

I held up the love letter, not particularly safely tucked inside its confetti-thin envelope.

"She doesn't know about a letter between her own mum and dad?" said Seb. I could feel his eyes burning into the side of my face.

I wished he wouldn't do that. Look at me too closely, I mean. Just in case he could read the thoughts that had been slithering around in my mind just now.

"It was tucked in the back of an old wallet-holder thing." I shrugged. "I mean, I *will* tell her sometime. And I'll tell her about this too –"

I waved a hand hazily in front of me at the building.

"– just not now, in case it upsets her all over again."

And Mum generally seemed a bit edgy and tense lately, probably 'cause of her and Dad needing to get some work going to pay for the cottage that was still half a building site. It didn't help that the twins were running off like naughty puppies, regularly biting people and trying to kill each other.

Also, I hated to think that Mum had got more

stressed since the end of the summer holidays 'cause of me too. Sneaking off to that beach party in Sugar Bay, the night when old Joseph's House went up in flames with me and my friends still in it . . . that had kind of made Mum horribly jumpy about where I was and what was happening to me at all times.

(I suddenly thought back to her trying not to cry at the train station and felt kind of choked.)

"Still, it's going to be really brilliant if you can find out something about your grandad though. Your mum might be pretty blown away, right?"

"Right." I nodded.

But truthfully, being here now, I didn't know *what* I could find out about some long-ago boy known only as Eddie. That's why I'd called this my very mad, impossible secret plan. 'Cause when it came down to it, I hadn't a clue what I was doing.

What an idiot I was. . .

"Hey, I just thought; you know that big, flat part of the park that we came through – near the big fountain?" Seb suddenly said.

"Well, yeah," I said warily. A circus was setting up there when we wandered past. Lorries, caravans, trucks; vast, flat, striped tent; burly, surly guys carrying posts and mammoth-length guy ropes.

"It's the only place in this whole park," said Seb.

I waited a second, trying to figure out what he was saying. And this time I felt brave enough to look at him when he talked.

"A flat place, with no trees. . ." he continued, shrugging his rangy shoulders. "It's the only place that the fair could have been."

"Let's go back there now!" I announced, my heart starting to thunder wildly.

"Go where?" asked Frankie, rejoining us, tipping her head and her plaits sideways as she licked a swirl of ice-cream from around the edge of her cone.

"Back to the other side of the park. Where the circus is setting up," I said speedily, hoping we could set off now, if not quicker. I couldn't wait to look at that anonymous chunk of grassland again with a new eye.

"Funny, isn't it?" said Frankie, fixing me with a long look.

I thought she meant funny, like funny-the-circus-could-be-on-exactly-the-same-site-as-the-fairground all those years ago.

But Frankie hadn't heard that part of me and Seb's conversation.

Frankie had a different kind of funny in mind.

"Funny how that stutter of yours just comes and goes again," she said casually, but sounding a little bit . . . well, *cruel*.

What was *that* about? Was it 'cause of Seb being short with her? 'Cause he seemed caught up in talking to me for a couple of minutes there? Well, *I* hadn't been the one to invite him along today! And *I* couldn't help it if he was more interested in my secret mission than Frankie, Neisha, Parminder, Lauren and Eleni put together.

Y'know, all those years together . . . at Aunt Esme's, at playgroup, at primary, at secondary; loud, confident, loyal Frankie had been my number one protector. Shy little Stella; she'd fight the playground bullies tooth, nail and claw to stop them teasing me.

But now she had a boyfriend, maybe the rules had changed. Maybe love had changed *her*, and how she felt about *me*.

Well, stuff the Hollywood movies and the lovey-dovey love songs. Going by Frankie and Seb, going by Evie and Eddie, maybe true love wasn't necessarily good for you at *all*. . .

Chapter 8

Dead ends and split-second shocks

"Eat!" said Aunt Esme, while stroking my hair as if I was a pussycat.

(Wow – I'd love to see a cat with fur as ringletty as my hair. How cute would that be? Or maybe I'd just give Peaches a perm when I got back to Portbay. . .)

I didn't like to tell Aunt Esme that I wasn't hungry – Auntie V had taken me to the posh café in the middle of Highgate Woods this morning, before she headed off to have a meeting with one of her clients. ("He's been offered the lead role in *Chitty Chitty Bang Bang*, but won't take it unless they promise to paint his dressing room silver and install a mirror-ball," she'd sighed.)

"These banana fritters are fresh made for you, my sweetheart," Aunt Esme urged me some more. "Can't believe I let them burn yesterday, when you two were going off for your picnic . . . with *Seb*."

Aunt Esme said the last bit very pointedly, throwing a look Frankie's way. She had that "three's a crowd" phrase in her head, I was sure – Aunt Esme was very fond of phrases and sayings. Course she didn't realize that in the end Seb had turned out to be less of a crowd and more of a huge help. More help than Frankie had been. . .

"*What* picnic?" Lauren asked, peering out from under her long, sideways-swept fringe.

Lauren is lovely, but a bit of an airhead. It's not that she's dumb, exactly; it's just that she's sometimes lazy when it comes to important things like listening and thinking. Other people would have some silent thought along the lines of "Picnic? But weren't they going to Hackney for a nosey-round? Ah, of course it's a secret, and the picnic is a cover-up story. . ."

Lauren? Well, missing out the thinking bit nearly blew our cover, of course.

"*Yes*," Frankie growled at Lauren. "We went on a picnic yesterday. OK?"

"Ah, now, you need a big glass of milk with that, Stella darling," Aunt Esme insisted, oblivious to the secret, and oblivious to daggers being shot Lauren's way. "Any of you other girls want some milk?"

All the girls looked ready to say no, except for Frankie, who bellowed:

"Yes, they'd ALL like some!"

Aunt Esme shrugged and went off to the kitchen.

"But I *hate* m—"

"Shhh!" Frankie shushed at Lauren. "Let Mum go get us all a drink! It'll keep her out of our way for a couple of minutes!"

It was Tuesday, and on today's mood rollercoaster I was feeling mostly happy, guilty and confused. Happy, 'cause I just was (it somehow felt nice today, like I was properly part of the gang again); guilty, 'cause I'd been so cross with Frankie yesterday and she'd been nothing but warm and friendly since I arrived five minutes ago; and confused, because I couldn't figure out if I'd been overly-sensitive and just imagined her digging at me yesterday afternoon in the park, with that stammering stuff. . .

"So, how was Hackney?" Parminder asked us in a whisper. "Did you find out anything about your grandad, Stel?"

"Not a lot," I said with a shrug, though it had seemed to mean a lot yesterday. "I found the block of flats where my nana lived, when she met

Eddie. And we think we worked out where the fairground might have been."

More than that, I didn't know. But *something* had to come next; I just needed time to figure out what.

"Hey, listen!" Frankie suddenly said urgently. "Seb texted me late last night with a cool idea. There was a circus setting up in Victoria Park while we were there – it opens at the end of the week. So why don't we all go on Friday afternoon?"

While the other girls did a chatter of "yeah!"s, I felt my heart give a surge of pure joy. We'd be going back to the park; maybe I'd stumble across some other clue about Evie and Eddie! I had no idea how, but I'd worry about that later. All I wanted to do now was fling my arms around Frankie, and Seb too for suggesting it. But as Seb was a) not here, and b) someone else's boyfriend, I stuck with Frankie instead.

"You better get ready to give me an extra *big* hug, 'cause I've got another great idea for Friday!" Frankie said in a muffled voice, as I squeezed a cuddle out of her.

"What is it?" I asked, breaking free.

"Well, Friday's your last night, so I thought we could have a sleepover here! What do you think?"

My friends went mad, frantically babbling about what pyjamas to wear, what music to bring, how many giant-sized bags of crisps we'd need. But then I remembered Auntie's V's secret something.

"But I've been meaning to tell you, Frankie – Auntie V wants to take me and you out on Friday night – for a special treat somewhere. She won't tell me what though."

"Cool!" said Frankie, raising her dark eyebrows my way. "Well, we could still have a sleepover. We could do it on Thursday night instead!"

"Do what on Thursday night?" asked Aunt Esme, bustling into the room with a tray with six glasses of milk on board, striped straws stuck in them (I don't think she'll ever stop thinking of us girls being anything but six years old).

"Have a sleepover here. Is that OK, Mum?" asked Frankie, using her most charming, friendly voice, i.e. not the one she usually used with her mum.

"Course, Francesca! Your friends are welcome anytime! I'll cook some nice Caribbean food for you." Aunt Esme beamed.

"Thank you!" Parminder said politely, before turning to the rest of us. "But what d'you all fancy doing today?"

"Before any of you goes *anywhere*, you're going to drink your milk and eat some banana fritters," Aunt Esme ordered us good-naturedly. "I know how you girls get so excited to be together that you forget to feed yourselves!"

Like good little six-year-olds, we did what we were told, and *almost* managed not to giggle till Aunt Esme was out of the room. . .

"I still feel sick," grumbled Lauren. "I *hate* milk."

"Just don't be sick *here*," said Parminder, pointing to the stall of black, fingerless, lace gloves and trays of bizarre jewellery. "You'll probably get charged, and all this weird stuff isn't cheap!"

We were at Camden Lock Market, which was always our absolute favourite place to hang out and shop and people-watch. The market's a jumble of old Victorian buildings and like a maze to wander through. There are hundreds of stalls packed in every building, and hundreds more lining every courtyard and winding alleyway between buildings. You can buy the coolest T-shirts, the freakiest rubber and lace goth gear, the most gorgeous food, and the strangest knick-knacks you never knew you wanted.

I was buying some of those strange knick-knacks

for my friends back in Portbay right now. (See? I *was* thinking about them, even if I'd been too busy to get back their texts and messages.)

"'Scuse me," I said to Frankie, who was standing in the way of the skull-and-crossbones key rings I was trying to check out.

"Soz. . ." mumbled Frankie, distractedly texting away on her mobile.

"Stella, *please* tell me you're not buying that!" Eleni shuddered, as I picked out one of the key rings and handed it and a fiver to the well-pierced stallholder.

"Tilda will love it!" I laughed at her.

Just like Amber would love her orange polka-dot rubber duck, Rachel would be chuffed with her make-up mirror with kiss prints on it, Megan would laugh at her punk in a snow-globe, and TJ would go mad for his "Dogs Rock!" mug.

"Hey, Stella!" said Neisha, appearing by my side and tugging impatiently at my sleeve, like a toddler about to pester her mum for a Mini-milk.

"What's up?" I asked, as I got my gift and my change.

"You're stuck, aren't you?"

"What? Gum *again*?" I said, checking my shoes. "I forgot everyone in London is so scuzzy when it comes to spitting their gum everywhere. . ."

"Nah!" Neish frowned at me. "I mean, with finding out more about your grandad, I mean?"

I'd admitted that on the way here. Maybe I'd hoped that my friends might come up with some ace ideas, but they were as stuck down the dead end of ideas as I was. (And Frankie was too busy texting to bother thinking.)

But I guess with having *no* address, and not even having a last name for Eddie, it wasn't going to be easy. Or even *possible*, I'd started to worry as we walked.

"Well, how about trying that?"

I turned round to see what Eleni was pointing at. It was a doorway that led up to another floor; and from the big sign by the doorway, all that lurked on the third floor was a tattoo parlour.

"What, you think I should get 'Where are you Eddie?' tattooed on my forehead or something?" I grinned at her.

"No, not the tattooist! *Underneath!* Look – tarot reader! Maybe they could tell you where to find your grandad!"

Neisha looked frantically enthusiastic, hopeful, I think, of coming into watch and getting thrillingly spooked.

"But I don't really believe in tarot readers." I shrugged, thinking of Madame Xara on the seafront in Portbay, who spent half her time telling people much the same fortune and the rest of her time working next door in the Cheese Please! cheese shop.

"Yeah, you don't believe in tarot readers," snorted Frankie, with a grin a mile wide, as she finally looked up from her text-a-thon. "But you believe in psychic cats and ghostly old ladies, don't you, Stel!"

I had to laugh at how dumb I must sometimes seem. But it was true; Peaches and Mrs S-T, and even the swooping psycho seagull who used to stalk TJ . . . I'd trust an appearance by any of them any day, but not someone who said their job was to look into the future.

"Don't you think it's worth a try, though?" Neisha tried to egg me on, seeing her chance of sitting in on something spooky slip away.

"Nah, I really don't—"

"At last!" shrieked Frankie, drowning me out. "Where've you *been*? You never got back to my last two texts!"

"Frankie, *you* said 'we're beside the freakshow goth jewellery stall'," I heard Seb tell her. "But there are about a *million* freakshow goth jewellery stalls, you muppet!"

Seb. Frankie had invited him *again*. She couldn't

seem to stop herself – having him near her, I mean. But who could blame her, I supposed. As I found out yesterday, he was every bit as kind and friendly as I'd hoped he was when I had that vast crush on him.

"Sheesh, what's *that*?!" He winced, shaking off Frankie's entwining arms and leaning over to gape at a tray of eyeball rings by my elbow.

"Gruesome?" I suggested, hoping the stallholder was too busy with new customers to hear me.

Seb smirked, and gave a jokey shudder.

"So, what's new? Got any more clues about Eddie and Evie?" he asked as he straightened up.

The answer was no, of course. But before I got the chance to say it, I spotted Eleni and Parminder exchanging glances.

What was that all about? I couldn't tell, but it made a little cloud float over my head, even though sunlight was flooding in the nearby window of the crowded building we were in.

"Say, what do you think, Stella?" I heard Seb suddenly ask.

Flicking my head around, I found myself staring into a large black-edged mirror on the wall behind the stall. Seb's face was in the mirror too, and he was holding two eyeball rings up to his eyes.

Little black cloud or not, I couldn't help

bursting out laughing. And then Seb took the rings away and grinned into the mirror too.

And I froze.

Seb's hair wasn't so afro, but his skin was darker than mine. My shock of curls was no bouffant, but my very light brown skin seemed bleached lighter with the sun streaming in directly at me.

Somehow in that fleeting second, with all the chaotic, brightly coloured stalls behind us, we almost looked like another teenage couple.

Another teenage couple in a black and white photo propped up by the lamp in Auntie V's spare room. . .

Chapter 9

A Mary Poppins moment

"And that plonker there is your dad. . ."

At fourteen, Auntie V looked like a skinnier, slightly punkier version of herself, in a striped top, black vinyl mini and flat, red suede boots that rumpled round her ankles. Her bright blonde hair was longer than it was now, with brown tips at the end; she looked like the girl out of Blondie, one of Dad's favourite bands from the 70s.

My dad, aged thirteen, looked like a bin.

"Why was he doing that?" I asked, peering at the photo in the album we were going through. Dad was mostly encased in an old-fashioned metal rubbish bin, with only his legs sticking out, baseball boots on show, and one long lace undone.

"His friends bet him he wouldn't do it, so of course he *did*, the big dope. He smelled rotten afterwards. I told him so and he ended up chasing me practically into the field behind the house!"

How funny; all I could see of Dad's friends was

one hand coming in to view at the side of the shot, thumb aloft. And there was Auntie V right behind the bin/Dad, with her arms folded and a weary look on her face. Thanks to the camera, she was trapped motionless in that one forever moment; yet twenty-eight years ago, she was just seconds from being chased giggling and screaming round Granny and Grandad Stansfield's rambly country garden.

Speaking of moments. . .

This afternoon: me and Seb. How totally bizarre that our reflection had suddenly reminded me unsettlingly of two someone elses, in some other time completely. Did this mean my mission was on the right track? Or was it just a trick of the light?

I hadn't known what to say, or even if I could actually *move*, I was so stunned – till a black-lipsticked goth helped me out by unceremoniously shoving me to one side, so she could see in the mirror whether a fanged bat choker went well with her *Die, Barbie, Die!* T-shirt. (It did.)

After that, the strangely strange moment was gone, even if I couldn't quite forget the trick our reflection had played on us, *or* the strange look Eleni and Parminder had given each other just before it. But even both of *those* odd thoughts started to blur by the time we went for food at a Vietnamese stall, where we had a competition to see who could actually eat their food *with* chopsticks, and *without* dropping any on the floor or down their front.

We all came out badly (though Parminder won on the technicality of being marginally less messy than the rest of us). Still, apart from looking like we'd been in a food fight and lost, it was good to have a laugh, and not get hung up on head-throbbing thoughts about what that mirror moment might have meant.

I needed time to work that out, and without Peaches or Mrs S-T giving me clues, it was taking my poor, befuddled brain ages to mull stuff over. Not that I had the luxury of time – it was Tuesday night already, and my secret mission wasn't exact going amazingly well. . .

The sudden ringtone of Auntie V's phone made both of us jump, even though it was set to a low, melodic burble.

"Better get it," said Auntie V, springing up from the sofa. "Could be work."

I turned another page of the photo album as she said hello, and then realized I didn't want to look at this slice of her and my dad's teenage life without Auntie V's funny and sarcastic running commentary.

"Going to my room for a sec," I mouthed at her, getting up.

"Mr Mirror-ball!" she mouthed back, pointing to the phone and pulling a face.

The softness of the expensive pale carpet squidged deliciously between my toes as I padded out of the living room, across the small hall and into the spare room. I went to close the heavy, cream, swishing curtains when something about the night-time view made me stop.

I was having another moment.

A sort of Mary Poppins moment.

No, I don't mean I about to burst into a chorus of "Supercalifragilisticexpialidocious", or use magic to tidy up the room (though that would have been helpful – I'd made it look like a bit of a tip in only four days).

It was more about – *all* about – that romantic, old-time vision you get of London at the beginning of *Mary Poppins*. Rambling old rooftops and chimney stacks, smoke swirls and church spires, spreading endlessly into the distance.

I was gazing out at a stunningly similar scene right now.

Auntie V lives right in the heart of Highgate,

where the houses are fearsomely historic – one hundred, two hundred, even *three*-hundred-year-old buildings are the norm. The stars in the sky might have more competition than in the old days, now that there were beams of electric lights instead of the duller glow of gas lamps, but the scene I was looking at was pretty much as it had always been, for a couple of centuries at least.

In *Mary Poppins*, you felt as if you could almost smell the soon-to-be-sleeping city, with its sweet wood and tarry coal fires burning in every grate.

Quickly wrenching the stiff sash window open, I took a deep breath . . . of nothing much apart from chilly air.

I had a sudden sharp yearning – not so much for Mary Poppins's London, which probably smelled of horse dung and bad sanitation anyway – but *another* window, in *another* bedroom, in *another* town.

In Portbay, late at night, I often sat for ages on the floor by my open window, gazing out at the deep, dark ink-blue of the sea, where it met the only slightly less dark blue of the sky on the horizon. Multi-coloured strings of lights glinted from the prom, and the senses-tingling scents of sea saltiness and jasmine drifted in with the breeze – mixing with a waft of peaches 'n' cream if my strange, fat cat happened to come sauntering along the garden wall, on to the kitchen roof and in through the open window, thanking me with a purr for the short cut.

I got distracted by a flutter.

A flutter of papery something.

I turned to see that the photo of Evie and Eddie had blown off its perch by the lamp on the bedside table.

Picking it up, I gazed at the two faces again, and felt my stomach do a forward roll at the way the heads tilted together, almost touching, same as mine and Seb's had for that split-second today.

It could mean one of three things:

1) It was some kind of sign that I was closer to finding out more about Eddie than I realized.
2) Something might happen between me and Seb (urgh...it made feel wildy uncomfortable just thinking that in the privacy of my own head).
3) I was cracking up.

I let my gaze dart to the gloomy theatre poster on the wall, but the pair of green cat's eyes seemed dull and lifeless tonight, so no help there.

"Stella. . .!" Auntie V's voice drifted through. "I've finished my call! D'you want to come back through? I could break out the strawberry cheesecake while we snigger at your dad some more!"

"Sure!" I called back. Who could resist an offer like that?

With a shiver, I tugged at the window, ready to close it – and saw the glint of two almond-shaped eyes staring up at me, from the darkened garden three floors down. They disappeared for a split-second in a blink, and then disappeared for good as the cat-sized shape slunk off on some night-time feline manoeuvre.

OK, so I didn't know what that meant exactly, but I knew it meant *something*.

With a warm glow inside me, I headed off to the living room and Auntie V, humming "Supercalifragilisticexpialidocious" under my breath. . .

Chapter 10

"Please text b4 it's 2 late. . ."

Wednesday: halfway through my week in London.

Searching: what I really wanted to be doing with my time.

Shopping: what I was *actually* doing with my time, thanks to being out-voted by my friends.

("What's the point in going back to Hackney today?" Frankie had frowned at me this morning. "We're going there on Friday, to the circus, so you can have a mooch around the park then!")

Hi – me + mates have been in the huge TopShop in Oxford Circus 4 3 hours now. 1st hour fun. 2nd hour OK. 3rd hour my mind is melting with boredom. Please text help b4 it's 2 late. . . luv Stella x.

"What are you doing?" asked Neisha, about to try her twenty-millionth top of the day on over her T-shirt.

"Just saying hi to everyone back home and

Megan," I explained, without feeling the need to recall exactly what I'd said apart from hello.

Well, what could I say? *My* mind might be turning to molten jelly, but all my friends seemed to be having the best time in the known universe, trawling round and round and round again, comparing this top with that, and this money-off tag with some special 2-for-1-and-you-get-the-third-half-price offer or whatever.

"What did you write to them?" Neisha pushed me some more.

Ooh, I hated straight out questions.

And ooh, I hated lying.

"Just hi, and sorry for not getting back to them sooner," I fibbed.

I glanced at Neisha's reflection in the long mirror and saw her moving a lollipop from one side of her mouth to the other, so the stick wouldn't get jammed in the material of the top she was hauling over her head.

"Hmm," mumbled Neisha distractedly, now turning this way and that way to check out the look. "D'you think this suits me?"

"Yes," I lied again quickly, kind of snow-blind after three hours looking at clothes, and totally incapable of telling one top from another by now.

"Wheeee!" squealed Lauren, practically running

towards us, waving something in her hands. "I think I've found it! This is *exactly* what I've been looking for!"

A belt.

A boring black belt with a plain silver buckle.

Kill me now. . .

"Wow, you've wanted one just like this for *months*!" gasped Neisha, as if Lauren was holding up a pair of trainer socks made out of genuine spun gold, trimmed with fine-cut diamonds.

"Er, Parminder's waving at me," I suddenly interrupted. "I'll go see what she wants."

A fib, if ever I said one. Parminder was over by the jeans, her head bowed in concentration as she compared infinitesimal differences in shades of denim blue.

Bleep!

I pulled my phone out of my pocket as I strode towards the jeans section.

How 2 relieve boredom? Think of me stuck in café, serving a coach load of old ladies who r really grumpy with me coz we've run out of scones. . . Amber x

"What's making you smile?"

"Huh?" I glanced up to see I'd arrived at Parminder's side without realizing it.

"Just a text from Amber," I said, flipping shut

the phone and shoving it away. "Decided on your jeans yet?"

It felt like Parminder was staring at me for a second, but she was probably just thinking about jeans.

"I've got six pairs I'm going to try on," she replied. "Do you think they'll let me in with six pairs?"

"I don't know," I said, gazing at the mound of identikit denim in her arms.

"Do you want to come with me while I try them on, and tell me what you think?"

If I'd been mouthy (like Frankie), I might have said what I felt, i.e. "I'd rather eat that rack of vest tops over there". Instead I thought of something that didn't seem so rude.

"I'm really, really thirsty. How about we all meet in the café in ten min—"

Bleep!

Another boredom-busting text from one of my friends, I hoped.

Take yr mind off boredom with this: I am SO jealous of you being in TopShop that I want to kill you!! Love Rachel x

Pity tele-transportation hadn't been invented yet, or me and Rachel could swap places for a bit. Sure, she'd love to glide around all the different floors, mooch at all the designer ranges, study all the endless reams of accessories. Me? I'd quite like to paddle in the sea. Or maybe have a walk up to the headland overlooking Sugar Bay, and pretend Joseph's House was still there. . .

"That was just—"

I was about to explain to Parminder, but she'd already ambled off, laden down, in the direction of the changing rooms, waving at Eleni and Lauren to come and help her.

Since I wasn't really thirsty, I didn't immediately take the escalator down to the next floor, where the café was. Instead, I thought I'd better find Frankie and let her know my loose plan to meet everyone there.

Course, I could have just called her on the mobile, but after three hours of taking baby-steps round rack upon rack upon rack, I felt like stretching my legs, and set off two steps at a time on the "up" escalator.

Frankie was last seen heading off to that floor, where the mega-vast, mega-flavoured range of jellybeans had tourists gawping and drooling. She wasn't buying them for herself; they were a present for Seb (of course), who couldn't come today 'cause he was playing his re-scheduled game of football.

Lucky Seb, to miss all this, I thought, as I hopped off at the top and stood on firm ground.

Though I kind of missed him. While everyone was cooing over black belts and endless tops, maybe me and Seb could've sat and chatted in the café. Maybe he could have inspired me now that my secret mission seemed to have ground to a halt.

Bleep!

Bored? Make like a dog. Find a cosy corner, curl up and go to sleep. Woof, Bob (lick)

That was TJ, in the guise of a big, hairy Alsatian who could use a phone keypad. Wow, I missed him, I suddenly realized. (TJ, I meant, not Bob.) He'd been my first living, breathing proper mate in Portbay, if you didn't count Peaches (the cat), Mrs S-T (the maybe-ghost) and Joseph's House (plus all the ghosts I'd imagined in it).

And he was my first ever *boy* mate, since I'd always found boys *especially*, stammeringly hard to talk to.

Maybe Seb could be my second ever boy mate?

"Boo!" Frankie shocked me with a grin. "What're you daydreaming about, Stella?"

It didn't seem like a good idea to say "your boyfriend", so I just laughed and shrugged and said I couldn't remember.

"Where's everyone else?" she asked, swinging her paper bag of jellybeans in her hand.

"In the changing room downstairs. Parminder's trying on—"

Bleep!

Another Portbay friend, I guessed. Another idea to make me smile, I hoped.

"Who's it from?" asked Frankie, as I skim-read the message.

"Tilda," I smiled, quickly rereading her ace suggestion.

"What's up?"

I didn't have to tell her about the boredom moan. But I *could* tell her the funniest boredom-busting idea any of my Portbay friends had come up with yet.

"What if I dared you to do something stupid?" I asked Frankie.

Frankie's eyes lit up. Like the thirteen-year-old, bin-wearing version of my dad, she could never resist a dare. . .

"Ta-naaa!"

Frankie was dressed completely in yellow, from a bandanna on her head to legwarmers round her ankles.

"You look like a banana," said Parminder, who

99

was wearing seven different pieces of clothing in seven different colours.

"*Exactly*," nodded Frankie. "Therefore I *am* the winner, and you all owe me the biggest slice of cake in the café!"

"Who says you're the winner?" said Parminder, putting her hands on her purple-trousered hips. "What about me and Stella?"

"Well, I know Stella's trying to be a star, but that's kind of cute, rather than terrible."

I was kind of touched when Frankie said that. I'd actually tried to look tacky, choosing the glitziest, sparkliest, most sequinned tat I could find and throwing it all together. Not that I was worried about winning Tilda's get-everyone-to-find-the-worst-outfit-possible-and-try-it-on competition. I was just pleased to be having a laugh and not having my mind turned to mush by shopping boredom any more.

"And as for you –" said Frankie, her eyes running up and down Parminder in mock disgust, "I don't know what you're supposed to be!"

"A rainbow!" sighed Parminder. "Isn't it obvious? Red and yellow and pink and blue, orange and purple and green!"

From behind a curtain in another changing cubicle, Neisha burst into song.

"'. . .*sing a rainbow toooooo!*'" she crooned, deliberately off-key.

"Shut up and get out here!" Frankie ordered her happily.

I was amazed. I thought the girls would be kind of reluctant to break off from their heavy-duty shopping addiction to act daft. But once me and Frankie had caught up with them, they'd straight away got into the idea, and shot off in all different directions to bagsy the worst outfit possible.

"Beat this!" yelped Neisha, throwing open the canvas curtain and striding out to greet us.

Furry moon boots, a trilby, rosebud-printed pyjamas and a lime-green bra and pants set worn over the top. It wasn't a look she'd be wearing home on the number 27 bus, *that* was for sure.

"I like it. Well, I *don't* like it, but that's the point," smirked Frankie. "What about you, Lauren?"

"In a sec!"

"Come on!" urged Neisha, at the top of her voice. "Let's see how naff you look!"

"Neish! *Shush!*" giggled Parminder, pointing to a shark-eyed shop assistant who was glancing down the row of cubicles to see which dumb bunch of teenagers were fooling about now.

Like a set of synchronized swimmers, we all

darted back into our cubicles, stifling the giggles to no effect.

"Is it safe?" whispered Lauren, after a few sniggering seconds. "Can I show you?"

"Yeah, it's safe," said Frankie, sticking her head around into the long changing room corridor. "Go on!"

Lauren stepped out of her cubicle with difficulty.

It was the six sets of trousers that made it tricky, I guess.

"They go from size ten to size twenty," she explained, as we all slapped our hands over our mouths.

She looked ridiculous, like one of my little brothers flap-books where you can mix-and-match the penguin's head with the zebra's stripy body and the crocodile's tail. From the waist up, she was regular Lauren. Glance further down, and six waistbands vied for attention as she grew bigger and bigger.

"And *why* did you think the princess tiara and wand went with that?" Frankie croaked, barely able to get the words out for laughing.

"Dunno!" Lauren shrugged vaguely. "So do I win?"

"Definitely!" I said, looking round at the other

girls who were nodding in between laughing. "Name your cake!"

Bleep!

"Got to get it," I said, diving back into the cubicle where my denim skirt was chucked on the floor, and rummaging in the pocket for my phone. "Might be one of my mates!"

Grabbing the mobile, I straightened back up, leant against the door frame, and read my message.

Bored? How about running through the store shouting "Cheese!!" really loud? Love, love, love Megan ;c)

Dippy Megan, with a typically dippy (and very embarrassingly) mad idea.

I grinned, imagining her cartwheeling across the sands in Portbay, that first day I met her. When she crashed into me, I mean.

"Who's it this time?" asked Parminder, making me glance up from the message-screen.

"Just Megan." I smiled, closing my phone and chucking it gently back on to my pile of clothes on the floor. "She cracks me up, sometimes."

"How come?" Neisha quizzed me.

The stuff Megan said and did; it would probably sound . . . sort of *lame* if I tried to describe it. You really had to meet her to understand.

"Ah, you wouldn't get it," I shrugged, not wanting to get tongue-tied and have my London buddies thinking my Portbay mates were naff or something. "Anyway, shall we get changed?"

"Yeah," came a flattish sounding mutter from a couple of the girls.

I suddenly realized they'd weren't looking so smiley any more.

And they were all looking at me, till Eleni and Parminder swapped one of their glances again.

My mood rollercoaster suddenly went into freefall. . .

Chapter 11

Spooky AND cool

"Are you being a good boy, Jake?" I asked.

"Yes," said a small voice, breathing heavily down a phone that was being held too close to a mouth.

"Is Jamie being a good boy too?"

"Yes."

"Ask him if Jamie's bitten anyone lately. . ." Auntie V said dryly, without looking up from the magazine she was flipping through on the sofa.

"Has Jamie bitten anyone today?" I checked.

"Yes," came Jake's reply.

"Who?"

"Yes."

Maybe he wasn't holding the listening part of the phone near enough to his two-and-a-half-year-old ear.

I decided to speak louder, and leave the biting subject alone.

"Are you being nice to Peaches?"

"Yes."

He'd *better* be. Jamie too.

"And are you boys staying out of my room?"

"Yes."

"And my den in the garden?"

"Yes."

"Do you miss me?"

"Yes."

Every yes had sounded the same. Even so, Jake answering yes to that last question made me feel wobbly somewhere in the middle of me.

"Need a poo, Stewwa. BYEEEE!!!"

Thunk! *Brrrrrrrrrrrrrrr. . .*

"What's up?" asked Auntie V, glancing up to see me staring at the phone.

"Jake hung up on me because he needed a poo."

"Oh, please . . . spare me the details!" Auntie V grimaced, hiding her face behind her magazine.

As soon as I put the receiver down, intent on dialling my home number again, the phone suddenly burbled into life, making me jump.

"Hello?" I said, half expecting to hear Jake say he'd changed his mind and only needed a wee, and half-expecting a slightly mad actor demanding to speak to my aunt and get her to sort out his silver paint swatches or whatever.

"Stella!"

Mum's lovely, familiar, warm voice.

"Sorry about that – Jake put the phone down before I could stop him. Oh, hold on. Andy – can you go with him? He might not find the potty in time. . ."

Oooh, I didn't miss those dual potty-training accidents. Though tonight, I really *did* miss my messy, muddled-up family. Some kind of heartstring in my chest vibrated badly, and suddenly I wondered if I should just come clean to Mum, tell her about Evie's stuff that I'd brought with me, and about my stalled search for Eddie.

But then it might make her sad again, and she wasn't sounding sad right now, just a bit bedtime-with-twins hassled. And anyway, if I told her that I'd trekked across to Hackney with Frankie (and Seb), she might start getting worried, or cross, or both.

And what was the point of bringing it up anyway, since I'd only seen a building, and a place in Victoria Park where the fair *might* have been? And exactly *nothing* else.

"Sorry, honey. So . . . are you having a nice time seeing Frankie and the girls?"

"Yes," I answered, though overall, it was more a case of yes, no, yes, no, yes, no. . .

"And is Esme well?"

"Yes," I replied, thinking of her obsession to fill us full of banana fritters this morning (maybe that's where Frankie got the idea for her worst-dressed choice in TopShop's changing rooms this afternoon?).

"What've you all got planned for tomorrow, then?"

"Yes. . . I mean I'm not sure yet," I mumbled, realizing I must've been sounding a lot like a more-grown-up, girly version of Jake.

"MUUUUUUUMMMMMMMMMYYYYY!"

"Oh, hold on, Stella. Andy – what's Jamie doing?"

From some muffled somewhere in the distance, I could here my dad shouting, "I'm trying to deal with poo, Louise – I don't know what Jamie's up to!"

"MUMMMMMMMYYYY! I FEEL SICK! I ATE LOTSA PLAYDOUGH!!"

"Listen, Stella," said Mum's slightly panicked voice, "I'll have to –"

"– go. I know," I finished the sentence for her. "I'll call you tomorrow."

"Tomorrow. Love you, baby."

Love you, baby: it's what she said to the boys, who *were* babies. But I kind of liked it a lot, when she said it to me just now. . .

"Why the long face?" asked Auntie V, dropping her magazine on to her lap as I placed the receiver back on to the unit. "Long faces only look good on horses."

I didn't want to mention the fact that talking to Mum made me ache for home. Mainly because it might make me cry, or worse still, stammer. So I said something else.

"Mum was just asking what I was doing tomorrow." I flopped down on to the square, not-particularly-comfortable armless white armchair. "But I'm not sure. I mean, Frankie and the girls want to go shopping *again*. To Islington this time."

I thought of our bus ride home together from the West End this afternoon: everyone seemed to get over the unspoken weirdness in the TopShop changing rooms pretty quickly, and were chattering away as usual in the back seats on the no. 27. Well, everyone apart from me. Although I kept smiling and nodding, I didn't feel like speaking up in case any stammering got in the way. So when Frankie, Neisha, Parminder, Eleni and Lauren started talking about how excellent it would be to go check out the shops round Upper Street and Essex Road, I said nothing, instead of what I *really* wanted to say, i.e. "Do we have to?"

"Well, Islington *is* nice for shopping," shrugged

Auntie V. "And I like a lot of the original buildings round Islington Green. Have you ever been to that wonderful, authentic retro-style diner? I forget its name. . ."

It didn't matter what its name was. Frankie and everyone just wanted to shop, and if we squeezed in time to eat, it would be at some fast food place.

"What's up, Stella? I'm guessing you're not interested in shopping?"

I shook my head.

"Well, why don't you suggest something else to your friends?"

"Like what?" I shrugged hopelessly.

"Like . . . like the Natural History Museum in Kensington. They've got some new dinosaur exhibit there, I'm sure I read somewhere!"

I pulled a pained face. Me, I'd have really liked to go see a new dinosaur exhibit, and maybe Parminder would too. Maybe Eleni as well, actually. But Neisha, Lauren and Frankie? They'd just yawn. . .

"Madame Tussaud's then?" said Auntie V, with a raise of her pencilled-in eyebrows.

I could practically hear Frankie and Neisha scoff "For kids and tourists", and shook my head.

"How about the Transport Museum in Covent Garden . . . it's had a huge refit and must be amazing.

You can see the original tube train carriages from the eighteen-hundreds!"

I'd LOVE to go to that museum. In the future, on another trip back to London, with Mum and Dad and the boys (in restraints). But I knew, for sure, that it would be Boring with a capital "B" to my friends.

"The movies," Auntie V persisted. "There's got to be *something* on at the cinema – it's half-term!"

There was, but it was all little-dude films, for the under-fives and that was about it. So I shook my head again.

Auntie V tossed her head back on the sofa and seemed to be racking her brains for inspiration.

And then something must have clicked.

"Highgate Cemetery!"

"What?"

"It's just a few minutes away from here. It's fascinating! There are two halves – one that's more modern that you can just wander round on your own, and the other side that's all dark and ivy-strewn and Gothic. . ."

Auntie V said the last part with arm actions, all widened eyes and film-style narration.

"Yeah. . .?" I was thinking it sounded pretty amazing. I had a vague feeling I must have been there once with Mum and Dad when I was younger, but I couldn't remember for sure.

"You have to pay for the Gothic side, as it's a guided tour. But it's absolutely fascinating!"

Suddenly, I didn't care what any of my friends thought . . . this was something I *definitely* wanted to do, maybe just because it fitted into the history/mystery stuff I'd got into in Portbay. Or maybe it was 'cause the idea of graveyards reminded me that long-forgotten people, specially dead people (like Evie) and potentially dead people (like Eddie?), still had stories that were worth hearing.

"I'm going to text my mates now!" I announced, feeling so fired up that I stupidly tried to get up out of the less-than-comfortable armless armchair without uncrossing my legs.

Correcting myself before I fell over and ended up with carpet burns on my chin, I hurried off to the spare room.

On the bed, laid out, were TJ's dog mug, Tilda's key ring, Amber's rubber duck, Rachel's mirror and Megan's snow-dome punk. I'd been in the middle of rearranging and sorting out the presents I'd bought for my Portbay friends, plus Evie's precious perfume bottle and cheap fair-won fan, when Dad had called earlier and put me on to Jake. (I'd planned on packing them all safely away at the bottom of my case, instead of rifling among them when I needed to find clean pants and socks.)

With the bed otherwise engaged, I pulled out the skinny white chair tucked under Auntie V's antique wood desk. Who to text first with my aunt's great idea for tomorrow? My best friend, of course.

Fancy something different tomoz? How about Highgate Cemetery? Spooky AND cool! Stella x

As I sent that text off, I felt even *more* sure that the graveyard tour was what I wanted to do. Maybe it was 'cause it also reminded me of the week back in the summer when me and TJ and everyone stumbled first upon Elize Grainger's grave, and then childhood best friend (and family servant) Joseph's ivy-covered grave next to her.

Or maybe it was because I didn't know whether my grandad Eddie was alive or dead, and thought that drifting around an atmospheric cemetery might help me tune into a clue or two.

Bleep!

Wow – Frankie had come back to me already? That was quick. . .

Sounds amazing. But can't afford return ticket to London – ha! TJ. PS Who did you really mean to text?

How funny; when my brain ordered my fingers to text my best friend, my fingers immediately chose TJ's number instead of Frankie's. Maybe my subconscious was trying to tell me something.

But could TJ really be more of my best friend that Frankie these days?

It was probably just the distant "brrrrrr" of a faraway motorbike, but it almost could be mistaken for a purr, a purr coming from the bundle of robes at the foot of the *Médée* poster. . .

Chapter 12

How to stomp all over a good idea

Like a secret garden, a secret world even.

The tour guide pointed out stone angels peering out from tangles of ivy; ornate, worn headstones looming out of the woods; an amazing avenue of Egyptian-style Victorian family vaults that looked like something out of one of those old *Indiana Jones* movies. I could've stayed all day listening to the stories of all the fascinating people buried there, from writers to wrestlers, from artists to circus owners.

But of course I couldn't stay all day. I couldn't even stay till the end of the guided tour. Mainly because we'd been asked to *leave*. . .

"Tighter, Stella! C'mon!"

Frankie was hunkering down, keeping her head low as I spun the swing she was perched on, the chains grinding as they meshed together.

Flash back six years, and we'd've been doing much the same thing, with various mums and dads in the playground smiling at our kiddy game, and the squeals we made when the wound-up swing went swirling round at hyper-speed.

The only difference now was that the few parents here on this chilly October day were tutting at the teenagers "fooling about" on the children's play equipment.

Oh, and the other difference was that on the six trillion visits we'd made over the years to the play park on Parliament Hills, I'd been more than happy to be chief spinner to my best friend. This time, though, I'd happily have kept winding till she was screwed up in a tiny girl-and-chain *knot*. . .

"Yay! Seb!!" Neisha called out from the top of the climbing frame, where she was sitting dangling her legs along with Lauren. "Frankie – it's Seb!"

"Lemme see him!" gasped Frankie, as she struggled to get free of the seat. You'd think she hadn't seen him in decades, instead of two days.

I let go and stood back, and the sheer velocity of the twisted swing chains sent Frankie spinning madly.

"*Aaaaaiiiiiieeeeeeeeee! Heeeeellllllppppp!!*" she laughed, gripping on tight and tossing her head back.

Seb didn't exactly rush to help. Instead he just moseyed in through the play-park gate, hands in his jean pockets, lopsided grin on his face.

As the swing juddered back and forth to a near stop, Frankie bounded off, her long skinny legs struggling to keep her upright. Arms outstretched like a comedy tightrope act, she weaved her way dizzily towards her boyfriend.

"Hey, nice moves – *not*!" we heard Seb tease her.

"Way to go, Frankie!" Eleni called out from the roundabout.

"Bet you two KitKats and a Mars Bar you fall over!" yelped Parminder, who was trying to push Eleni round as fast as she could.

"You're on!" Frankie called out over her shoulder, making herself wobble precariously.

Two KitKats and a Mars Bar – that was Frankie's favourite pig-out on bad days (i.e., at period time, or like the time she scored 9% in a chemistry test, and was told by our science teacher that it was an all-time record in low marks).

Seb stood still, his grin wide, his arms suddenly swinging open to catch Frankie as she stumbled towards him.

As she fell into him, Seb picked her up, spun

her around, then plonked Frankie firmly on her feet. Kissing the top of her head, I heard him say, "You muppet!"

"How was the football?" Neisha called out to Seb. "You ready to audition for the next England squad yet?"

"Yeah, the next England *tiddlywinks* squad, maybe! We were *rubbish*! Totally! Get this – we lost 8–0!" he moaned good-naturedly, as he came towards us all, one arm wrapped around Frankie, supporting her.

"Should have come with us to Highgate Cemetery this morning instead," Parminder told him, with a smirk playing around the corners of her mouth.

"Yeah? Wish I had. Least I wouldn't've been standing here, full of shame! So, how did it go?" he asked, now looking specifically at me.

How did it go? Hmmm. . . What should I tell him first?

Maybe that the nice American family in our group got seriously fed up with Frankie mumbling "Howdy, y'all!" every time one of them opened their mouth to ask the tour guide a question.

Maybe that Neisha and Parminder burst into unsubtle giggles every time Frankie "whispered" "Howdy, y'all!"

Maybe that Eleni and Lauren held on to each other and started squealing pantomime-stylee about how "scary" the place was, and that Lauren started snivelling at one point and said she was spooked and wanted to go home.

All the time, the tour guide watched us with a beady eye (she'd been wary of taking us in the first place, since Frankie and Neisha were harmonizing some old Sugababes' track as we waited in the office for the tour to begin).

I think the tour guide might just have put up with us, till Lauren screamed like she'd seen a legion of zombies when a fox shyly darted out from behind a gravestone.

It was then that the guide asked us to leave.

And it was then that Frankie sniped, "It was dead boring anyway!" as we walked away. (With me wanting to crawl into the nearest grave and die. . .)

"We got asked to leave!" giggled Frankie, before I got to put any of this morning's sheer embarrassment into words.

"Huh?" Seb frowned at her. "How come?"

"We didn't do anything!" Frankie protested, conveniently forgetting, well, *everything*.

"God, Seb, it was *sooooo* boring!" Neisha chipped in, from up on top of the climbing frame. "The tour guide just droned on and on and on about all these long ago whoevers buried there, like anyone nowadays cares!"

Neisha was smiling in a sweet way. She didn't mean to stomp over my good idea. Any day of the week, any week of the year, she would *never* deliberately set out to hurt anyone's feelings. But hey, my feelings were suddenly, *un*-deliberately hurt. Going to Highgate Cemetery was special to me; going there felt magical, reminding me of the churchyard in Portbay, where Joseph and Elize were buried. Going there reminded me of the overgrown, long-forgotten, pets' graveyard, just before the whole of Sugar Bay was lit up when the old, dry, neglected house burnt down. . .

"Anyone want anything from the café?" I asked, pretending to rifle through my purse, so no one could see the tears prickling in my eyes.

Unaware of my feelings (hey, that never happened in the old days), Frankie and Neisha and everyone garbled out their orders, as I started heading off to the further playground gate, in the direction of the park café.

They needed Diet Coke, they needed chocolate, they needed crisps.

And me? I needed to step away from a gang of girls who used to be as much a part of me as breathing and my stammer – but who now sometimes made me feel like a complete outsider.

As I walked away, two voices raged in my head. . .

How could they all embarrass me so much today!

Because a) they didn't mean to, and b) this stuff doesn't mean anything nearly so much to them as it does to me.

But over the years, I've listened to Neisha's awful R&B CDs and acted interested, and hid how mad I've felt when Eleni's trailed round seventy-five shoe shops till she decides to buy her new school shoes in the very first shop we were in. Why can't my mates behave better, when it's a special trip that I want to do?

Because it doesn't mean the same to them. They haven't been through what me and my friends in Portbay have been through. I've got to remember that.

Don't they get it, though? I haven't managed to find out very much about my Grandad Eddie, who might be dead, and going through a beautiful graveyard makes me feel somehow more connected to him.

So, trawling round a Victorian graveyard makes *me* feel connected to the grandad I've never met, whose family came from Barbados, who will probably be in his very spritely late-fifties, if illness and runaway trucks haven't got him. How are these girls meant to get that, since none of it's personal to them?

Maybe 'cause I just thought friends were meant to care about their mates' feelings. . .

"Yeah, how much is this lot?"

Oh. . .

I'd been concentrating so intently on the argument raging in my head that I hadn't noticed I was at the front of a sizable queue with five Cokes, three chocolate bars and four packets of crisps practically falling out of my arms.

The woman behind the counter switched her gaze from me to Seb, who I suddenly found standing beside me, counting money into her hand.

"W-w-what are you doing here?" I asked, confused and shy and wondering where Frankie was.

"It's just plain maths," shrugged Seb, taking his change.

"Huh?"

(I vaguely heard some tutting going on in the queue behind me.)

"Look, there're five of them and one of you; you can't carry all that stuff on your own. OK?"

he said, taking the cans and crisps from my hands, leaving me with only the chocolate to carry.

"I-I-I've got money here," I tried to offer him. "It's right h-h-h—"

"Whatever."

The way he cut off my stammer; the way he said "whatever" . . . it wasn't harsh, like you might think. It was gentle and friendly, as if he felt a bit sorry for me, and wanted to help me out.

That's it! I thought silently to myself, a sudden realization thunking me in the chest. *Seb feels sorry for me! And not just 'cause of my stammer; but 'cause he knows I used to have a crush on him! I bet Frankie couldn't stop herself from telling him once they were going out together!*

Thank goodness thundering heartbeats were silent to anyone outside your own body. . .

"Anyway, let's sort the money out when we get back to the others."

I didn't know what to say so I said nothing.

"Today didn't go so well, huh?" Seb turned and smiled at me, as we shuffled past a slightly impatient bunch of mums 'n' fretful toddlers waiting to buy their lattes and Mini-milks.

A very huge part of me was glad that Seb was here: the part that appreciated him being interested in Evie and Eddie, and appreciated him wishing (genuinely) that he could've been at Highgate Cemetery today instead of being beaten to a pulp in a football match with his mates.

Another fairly huge part of me wished he hadn't come to help me at all. I didn't want his pity, being nice to the "cute" stuttering girl who used to have a thing for him.

And what was Frankie going to make of him coming after me? Did she think – like the others – that I still might not be over him?

Was Seb's Good Samaritan stuff going to start off any of that weird swapping-glances thing between my mates? I mean, was Seb coming to help me going to make me feel even *more* of a stranger with my old buddies than I already did?

"It didn't go well," I answered his question, remembering the toe-curling moment when the tour guide had asked us to "Leave, please. *Now*." (Oh, the *shame*.)

"Maybe having six thirteen-year-olds was too much like being in charge of a school trip!" Seb smiled, in his endearingly cute, nearly fifteen-year-old, lopsided way.

"Maybe." I shrugged, not quite in the mood to forgive my badly-behaved supposed best mates.

"Well, forget about that stuff," said Seb.

Easy for him to say! said one of the argumentative voices in my head.

"'Cause today I just thought of something some guys in my year at school did a while back."

It was Thursday, my second last day in London, and so far my secret mission had got astoundingly, amazingly badly. I didn't know what Seb's mates could've done at school that would make my mood start clambering up that rollercoaster ride. . .

"Leon and Geroy both did these projects about finding out about their West Indian ancestors," said Seb, stopping to grab a packet of crisps that went tumbling from his arms. "They found out lots of stuff from some website."

"What's the site called exactly?" I demanded excitably, catching a Mars Bar that was set to slither out of my arms and make an escape.

I didn't care now that Seb might be being extra-nice to me 'cause he felt guilty or weird or something about me having that long-ago crush on him. All I cared about was finding a way to get closer to Eddie.

"Don't know . . . it wasn't the site I was using for my school project, so I don't remember. But I could try and find out for you, if you like?"

If I liked?

I didn't need any spook signs to tell me this was the best lead I'd had all week.

Plop!

"What? What's so funny?!" Seb turned around and smiled, wondering why I had stopped dead and dissolved into giggles at the large dollop of poo that had just been deposited at my feet by a low-flying, shouldn't-be-so-far-from-the-sea seagull.

"Nothing." I laughed.

Thanks for the spook sign, anyway! I said silently to the spiralling gull above my head. . .

Chapter 13

The sleepover, Seb and the big, bad silence

Two sleepovers, two different bunches of girls in their PJs, talking rubbish.

The first sleepover happened at the end of summer, in my newly decorated room in the cottage in Portbay, with TJ acting as an honorary girl for the night – though he had to suffer a bad night's actual sleep sharing my twin brothers' bedroom (think whiffy nappies, wailing and toy missiles).

The second sleepover was happening now, in Frankie's fuchsia-pink bedroom, with not a boy in sight – Aunt Esme would've put a determined foot down if Frankie had tried to wangle Seb here tonight.

I think it's kind of the law to speak rubbish at sleepovers, and so far we'd covered stuff like the worst biscuits ever invented (boring Rich Teas), celebs who looked liked animals (Dominic

Monaghan who played Charlie in *Lost* was a meerkat, we'd all agreed), and now we'd moved on to who we'd first fancied when we moved to the Rochester in Year Seven.

Frankie and Parminder had both liked Jonas Cale, but couldn't remember why. Lauren liked Jaz Singh, and still kind of liked him now. Eleni said she was too nervous of everyone in Year Seven to have a crush. Mine had been a boy called Sean Barlow, who I stopped liking the minute I heard him fart out loud in assembly.

Neisha had said Wayne Kwame, but Frankie wasn't letting her get away with that for a second, and confronted her with another name.

"You have *got* to be joking!" shrieked Neisha.

"You did too!" Frankie was insisting.

"I did NOT fancy Mr Durward!" Neisha said wide-eyed, her skin darkening.

"You said he had nice hair!" Parminder joined in with the teasing.

"Look, I *once* said that his haircut was quite cool – 'cause normally it was a disaster. That does *not* mean I fancied him."

Mr Durward was a gawky-but-kind geography teacher, straight out of teaching college when we were in Year Seven. Neisha seemed to have blanked the times we caught her staring at him and forgetting to write down what he was actually saying.

"You *fancied* him. You did, you did, you *did*!" Frankie laughed, grabbing a pillow and lashing out at a giggling Neisha with it. "And I'm going to keep on thumping you with this till you admit it!!"

"No! Ooff!" laughed Neish, holding her arms up to stave away the squashy blows. "Oh, OK, so I did a bit! But don't tell me *you've* never fancied anyone dodgy!"

"No I haven't actually," said Frankie, letting go of the pillow and hurling it at Neisha. "My track record shows my good taste in boys. There's been –"

I could sense a list coming on, the clue being that Frankie was now holding all her fingers up. I didn't need to hear who she'd had crushes on, as I'd lived through every one of them with her. And I knew it would somehow end up with her getting back to her favourite subject: Seb.

It was easier to be out of here and looking busy, to save all the stares that would be coming my way any second at the mention of his name. . .

I gathered up the empty plates as fast as I could, before Frankie had even got the second boy on her list, and stomped off down the corridor.

For a few minutes, I faffed around, rinsing bowls and plates in the sink, till Aunt Esme came bustling in from the living room.

"Bless you, but put that down, Stella my sweetheart! Just you get back to the fun!" she insisted, taking the tea towel out of my hands.

"I don't mind, really," I told her, happily stalling for time with the dishes.

"Hmm . . . sounds like a herd of baby elephants having a wrestling match," said Aunt Esme, frowning in the direction of Frankie's bedroom. "What are those girls doing in there?"

"Um, don't know."

The thumping and giggling made me think it might be a proper pillowfight now, which would be good news, as it meant Frankie's crush list was over with and I could safely go back into the bedroom.

"You're looking peaky. You OK, sweetheart?" asked Aunt Esme, grabbing me gently by the arm as I started to go.

"I'm all right." I shrugged and smiled, hoping that was a decent enough answer for her.

"Something's getting you down, isn't it? You tell your Aunt Esme, now," she insisted, patting the vinyl covered stool next to hers.

"It just . . . it's just that I thought being back would be great," I found myself saying, perching on the stool and crossing my arms over my stripy pyjama top. "And sometimes it *is* great, and sometimes it's sort of . . . not."

It was all I could say. I mean, I couldn't go telling her that Frankie and the others had acted really badly this morning and got us chucked out of the cemetery. And where would I start with the funny stares that happened sometimes, especially when the subject of Seb came up (and especially when I was walking back from the café with him this afternoon)?

"Ah, finding it hard to fit back in where you left off, honey?"

"Mmm."

"I know. You think nothing could change in such a short while, but it does, doesn't it?"

Aunt Esme patted my hand reassuringly as I nodded.

"And my Francesca is not helping, by dragging that boy around with her like a puppy wherever she goes. I tell her, 'Leave him be!', but her head is full of him, and she doesn't listen."

"Seb's all right," I tried to say in his defence. "He's been trying to help me."

"Help you how?" Aunt Esme asked, frowning in curiosity.

Yikes, I was veering horribly close to blurting out my very mad, impossible secret mission.

"Just by being friendly," I said, coming out with the first reasonable thing I could think of. "Listen, I'd better get back – I promised to bring through more juice."

I got up, grabbed the carton that was sitting on the draining board, and turned right slap, bang into Aunt Esme's arms.

"You may be feeling like a square peg in a round hole, Stella my sweetheart," Aunt Esme said quietly, "but don't let it stress you out. Just try remembering why you were all friends in the first place."

And why were we all friends in the first place? Well, Frankie and me grew up together, like sisters (her the confident one, me the horribly shy one). And then at Rochester, we'd hooked up with the other girls. But did they all want to be friends with fun Frankie, I suddenly wondered, and *I* just happened to come along as part of the package?

I think Aunt Esme's words were meant to

make me feel better, but instead they'd made me feel a little bit worse. . .

"Thanks," I tried to say with a smile. "Uh, I'd better take this through now."

Padding off down the corridor, I was sure I felt Aunt Esme's eyes boring into the back of my head. I only hoped she hadn't developed psychic powers in the last few months since we'd seen each other, or she'd know I would have been tempted to go straight out through the front door, if I hadn't been dressed only in stripy pyjamas and fluffy pink ankle socks.

"Surprise!!"

I nearly dropped the carton of juice as I walked back into that sudden, completely unexpected welcome.

Frankie, Neisha, Parminder, Lauren and Eleni were sitting in a circle on the floor, with all the furniture pushed right back to the sides of the room to make enough space. (Was *that* the baby elephants noise?)

In the middle of the floor was the upturned lid of a large box, and inside *that* was a circle of Scrabble letters and a small plastic figurine that looked like the sort of movie tie-in toy that you got free with your meal in McDonald's.

"What is it?" I asked, joining the girls on the floor.

It reminded me a bit of when me and my other friends all hunkered down in my room in Portbay, while Tilda tried out a few spells from a new book she'd got (and nearly set the house on fire with a candle while she was at it).

"We're going to do a pretend Ouja board, to see if we can try and find out about your Grandad Eddie!" said Frankie.

The other girls grinned and nodded. Now I felt bad, bad for being so angry with them today, and bad for hinting to Aunt Esme that things weren't as good as they could have been with them.

"I don't really believe in that stuff," I said, though I was smiling and feeling warm inside that the girls cared enough to help me in my mission. Even if it was in a stupid way.

"Yeah, *yeah*, Stella," grinned Frankie. "You just believe in psychic cats and whatever – we know. But you've only got one more day, and this was the best we could come up with. Stick the lights out, Parminder. . ."

"No!" squealed Eleni. "Leave the lights on!"

"OK, OK!" Frankie shushed her, reckoning, I supposed, that squealing and shrieking might bring her mum a-knocking on the door to see what we were up to.

"How do we start?" I asked.

"Everyone puts one finger on Chicken Little," Frankie explained, pointing to the plastic toy in the middle of the circle, "then you ask a question, Stella, and Chicken Little should start moving, spelling out the answer."

Gingerly, and giggling, we all put a finger out as she'd told us to. And now I had to come up with something to ask.

"Um . . . uh. . ." I stumbled, my mind flapping around for a straightforward question. "Is my Grandad Eddie alive?"

Chicken Little started to move. We all swapped glances and nervous smiles.

"It's going to 'Y' – the answer's yes!" gasped Neisha, as sure enough, "e" and "s" followed.

"I don't like this. . ." muttered Lauren, feeling like she might be about to pull her finger out of the finger pile.

"Don't you dare!" Frankie ordered her. "Everyone in the room has to do it, or it won't work. Ask another question, Stella!"

What did I want to know? Well, if Eddie was really alive, I wanted to ask what he'd done with his life, and if he ever thought of long-lost Evie, and a *million* other questions. But maybe I needed to ask an obvious one first. . .

"Where are you?"

"It's a 'B'!" said Eleni.

"Barbados!" exclaimed Parminder. "Your grandad's parents came from there originally, didn't they? He must have gone back!"

My heart was thumping like it was set to explode. Until I started to watch which *other* letters Chicken Little was busy spelling out.

"B . . . E . . . H . . . I . . . N . . . D," all us girls said practically in unison. "Y . . . O . . . U . . ."

"Huh?" I mumbled. "Behind you?!"

"BOOOOOO!!!" roared Frankie.

With assorted screams and shrieks coming from the bedroom, it was a wonder Aunt Esme didn't come running in with a frying pan to beat off the burglars she might have suspected were attacking us. Maybe she *was* on her way, and only stopped herself outside the door, pan above her head, when she heard the cackles of relieved laughter coming from inside.

"Gotcha!" Frankie beamed, pointing at me first, and then round all of the rest of our gang.

OK, so she'd played a trick on us all, but just laughing with the girls felt good, like the old times we used to have together. Maybe Aunt

Esme was right, I just had to remember why we were friends in the first place. . .

A ringtone warbled into life – it was the sound of Frankie's favourite track by Beyonce, so it was easy to guess whose phone it was.

"'Scuse me!" said Frankie, hopping on to her bed and grabbing her mobile off the window sill.

And from the grin on her face when she saw the display, it was easy to know who was calling.

"Hey, babes! How're you? Yeah? We're OK. I just got the girls good by playing this trick on them! I – huh? Oh. Oh . . . OK."

Frankie's broad smile faded away like an ice lolly in a microwave.

Uh-oh. What was wrong?

Suddenly Frankie's slim silver phone was under my nose.

"Seb wants to talk to *you*," said Frankie, in the flattest of tones.

"Um, right," I mumbled, taking the phone from her. "Hi. . .?"

I was aware of a big, bad silence radiating from my friends.

"Stella? Hi!" said Seb brightly. "Look – got to make this quick, my battery's about to pack up.

But I got some news – remember those lads I mentioned earlier? Leon and Geroy?"

"Mmmm," I mumbled, watching as Frankie now pretended to be engrossed in sorting through her CDs.

"Well, Leon got back to me. He says that website is something he got on to through Hackney Museum's site."

Hackney! I hoped the flush of excitement in my face didn't look like some kind of guilty blush to my friends, who were unsubtly sneaking glances my way.

"So, fancy going to Hackney Museum before the circus tomorrow? Maybe meet outside about one?"

"Absolutely!" I said, as I heard his line suddenly go dead, his drained battery cutting him short.

Buzzing. I was absolutely buzzing inside with thoughts and possibilities. Maybe *this* was the way out of the Eddie dead end I'd found myself in!

Gutted. I was absolutely gutted with how miserable and suspicious of me Frankie looked right now, as I handed her the phone back.

"Frankie, Seb just wanted to tell me something that might help me find stuff out about Eddie."

"Yeah? Great! Whatever . . . it's cool," she said

brightly, as if she wasn't the least bit bothered. "Wanna stick on this CD, Lauren?"

Maybe she thought I couldn't see, but I could.

Down by the floor, half-hidden under a pillow, Parminder was squeezing one of Frankie's hands, and Frankie was squeezing it right back.

When the lights finally went out, I had a feeling I might be spending the whole of this sleepover lying very, very awake. . .

Chapter 14

Real-life snakes and ladders

Think of a nanny in Britain in the olden days. It's Mary Poppins again, isn't it?

But there was another type of nanny back then, an ayah.

Ayahs were Indian women who worked for European families who'd been living out in India. The ayahs came over on the long sea journeys back to Britain, looking after families' children, and were then often abandoned once they got here.

On the display board I was reading, it said that it was common in the 1800s to see Indian women destitute and begging on the streets of London.

If only they'd had a little of Mary Poppins's magic to whisk them back home, I thought, as a tear escaped from the inside corner of my eye and trickled down my nose.

"OK, I just checked for you," said Seb, coming back to my side. "And the guy at the desk said that

140

the website my mates looked up is called movinghere.org.uk."

Quickly wiping away the drip on the end of my nose, I started scrabbling about in my bag, trying to find a pen and paper so I could scribble this info down.

"But there's not a lot of point making a note of it," said Seb, putting his hand in front of my notepad and squashing my hopes at the same time.

"Why not?"

"Well, the guy at the desk says they collect stories from all sorts of people who settle in Hackney—"

"Like people from the West Indies?" I interrupted.

"Yeah, and Asians, and Jews, and Vietnamese and Kurds and whoever," Seb continued. "And they pass the stories on to the MovingHere people, who collect them from all over."

"Well, *that* sounds good, doesn't it?" I said, still trying to hang on to a little piece of hope that this morning's trip wouldn't be a waste (apart from the fact that I'd learned the sad story of the ayahs).

And I really needed to know that coming here *mattered*. I'd nearly cancelled on Seb, only I didn't know his phone number and didn't dare ask Frankie. With her so tight-lipped with me already, I felt I had to find out *something* about Eddie, just to prove that today's trip was all about wanting to solve my mystery, not just to hang out with her boyfriend and bug her.

"But it's just all random people's stories, Stella," shrugged Seb. "Plus a how-to-trace-your-ancestors section."

"Brilliant!" I jumped in hopefully.

"But the problem is, you don't know Eddie's second name!"

It was a problem I'd tried to shove to the back of my mind during every second of me thinking about this very mad, impossible secret mission.

I don't know what exactly I'd hoped to find here at the museum; I think I'd maybe wanted to walk past displays of ancient longboats and facades of old Eel, Pie and Mash shops and suddenly see a poster for a travelling fair that pitched up in Victoria Park in the summer of 1965. I'd wanted to see accompanying black and white photos of the fair in full swing, with names and descriptions under each one. And most of all, I guess, I'd wanted to see a photo of a young, handsome black guy with dimples, working on a hook-a-duck stall where girls could win pretty paper fans.

And right beside that specific photo, I wanted to read a caption that said something like: "Eighteen-year-old Eddie Whoever, working here for the summer before getting a steady job and settling down for life at 48 Somewhere Gardens, This Town."

After thinking about the secret mission for weeks, and getting pretty much nowhere with it, I was tired out, and just desperately wanted an easy answer to come popping right up in front of me.

Of course, I was worn down too because of Frankie.

When I'd finally managed to explain my phone conversation to her and the girls last night, she'd tried to seem casual, saying she'd love to come to the museum too. And in the morning, over breakfast, when Aunt Esme reminded her she had a dentist's appointment, she'd gone into a mega-strop, leaving Aunt Esme open-mouthed, and the rest of us cringing.

"It's not you going with Seb," Frankie had tried to say, before I left. "It's just about Mum, forgetting to tell me stuff."

She was lying, I knew.

I only hoped she'd be in a better mood later, when we met up in Victoria Park. We'd agreed to get together beside the big, fancy fountain there, just before the circus was due to start.

Only that wasn't for another hour-and-a-half, I realized, looking down at my watch. With the trail gone cold so early at the museum, what exactly was there for me and Seb to do?

"I've got an idea. . ." Seb mumbled, that lop-sided grin appearing on his face.

"What?"

"We need to go to Cleveland House again."

"Do we?" I blinked, my stomach a tangle of not-daring-to-hope knots. . .

"I can't!" I whispered, a tsunami of shyness engulfing me again, just like it had when we were in the museum and I was way too scared to ask for help.

"Well, *I'll* do it," said Seb, just like he'd done in the museum, when he'd gone and done my talking for me. (It was weird, but I hadn't been like this in Portbay, where I'd had my photo taken so often at the museum – over stuff to do with Joseph's House – that it had started to feel like an extension of my home.)

"But how do you know which one?" I asked in

a panic, staring at the panel of buzzers by the entry door.

"Let's stand back a bit and check it out," said Seb, taking my cold, sweaty hand and leading me backwards up the path. "Now which of these flats looks like a sixty-ish plus person or couple lives in it?"

Seb's plan was to try and find someone who'd lived in the block for years, who might've known Evie, and even Eddie.

I let my eyes dart about the balconies and windows of Cleveland House.

"*That* one."

I was pointing to a flat with neatly trimmed window boxes of purple heather and pink cyclamen. On the balcony was a metal clothes horse with nice, neat cardies and sensible skirts hanging up to dry in the breeze.

"Right. . ." murmured Seb, mentally working out the floor and the flat, and walking forward to examine the buzzer panel again. "Number nine."

As he pressed his finger on the nine key, I froze in fear. How could he be sure?

"Hello?" an older lady's voice crackled through the box.

"Hello – sorry to bother you," Seb dived straight in. "I'm with a friend who is trying to find out about her grandmother, who used to live here at number twelve, back in the sixties –"

Seb looked at me, to check he'd got that right, and I nodded so stupidly hard that I felt dizzy.

"– and she's keen to talk to anyone who might have known her. Her grandmother's name was Evie Jones. You don't happen to have known her, do you?"

I waited to hear the buzzer click off, same as Seb's phone had done last night when the battery went on it. I mean, if *I* was an older lady and some young stranger pressed on my door like this, I'd be hanging up my entryphone and double-locking my door double-quick.

BZZZZZZZZTTTTTT *click!* went the entry door, gently swinging open.

"Of course I remember poor Evie – come on up," said the voice.

Seb and I glanced at each other, both stunned by our good luck.

And five minutes later, we were in Mrs Ornella Stanley's fearsomely tidy kitchen, each with a cup of very sugary tea in our hands.

"I was that little bit older than Evie, so we didn't mix, so to speak," explained Mrs Stanley. "I was newly married to Bruce –"

She nodded at the man in the living room, engrossed in a loud war film.

"– and had just moved in here around the time Evie was seeing . . . what was his name, again?"

"Eddie," I helped her out.

"Yes, Eddie."

"Did you know anything about her parents stopping her seeing him?" I asked, a whole lot braver now that I was finally getting somewhere.

"Well, I didn't know anything like that exactly," Mrs Stanley said, passing a plate of biscuits our way. "All I saw was that Eddie was gone, moved on with the fair. Then the Jones family were aiming to move out a while after, 'cause of Evie's trouble."

Mrs Stanley stopped short, looking at me in particular, gauging if she had spoken too frankly for someone of my age.

"I know about Evie being pregnant with my mum," I told her, so this gentle older black lady didn't have to feel uncomfortable telling me the facts.

"Well, they moved out once she started showing," said Mrs Stanley.

I nodded, to let her know I understood that "showing" was an old-fashioned way of saying the baby bump was getting noticeable.

"The family, they moved north to Leytonstone, I think. . ."

"Walthamstow," I corrected her.

"Ah, well, dear, you know as much as I do." Mrs Stanley smiled. "I'm sorry to hear that Evie died too soon, but glad to hear she had a lovely daughter – and grandchildren, even if she didn't get to meet them. I'm sure she'd be proud."

I blushed a little, and sensed the conversation seemed to be nearing an end. All that was left was for me to thank her.

"Course, it would have been nice to hear how Eddie had done in life too," Mrs Stanley suddenly said wistfully. "Such a nice, friendly, lovely young man. I did enjoy our conversations. . ."

"You *talked* to my grandad?!" I burst out.

Mrs Stanley paused, and peeked through at her engrossed husband.

"Oh, we had a chat a few times," Mrs Stanley said, lowering her voice so that her husband didn't get uncontrollably jealous of some teenage boy who might have talked to his then young, attractive wife all of four decades ago.

"What did you talk about?" Seb jumped in, as swept up in curiosity as I was by now.

"Oh, this and that. . ." Mrs Stanley said vaguely. "How he was only working the fair for the summer, because a pal of his was setting up a garage the next year and promised him a job then."

So Eddie was a trained mechanic, maybe? I knew people left school at fourteen back then and often went into apprenticeships, so that could fit.

"Can you remember anything else?" I asked hopefully.

"Not really. Only his nice smile, and the way he seemed so fond of Evie. . ."

It was more, much more than I'd hoped for, and I felt I could've hugged Mrs Stanley, if it hadn't seemed too forward for someone you'd only just met.

"Well—"

I'd just started to say my thank yous when Mrs Stanley began talking again.

"Oh, and we did chat one time about the ships our parents had come over from the West Indies on. Mine came from Jamaica on the SS *Auriga*, and his came from Barbados on the . . . now . . . can I remember what it was called?"

Please let her remember, I begged silently. If I had a ship's name, there would be records I could look up!

"It wouldn't help, Stella," said Seb, his mind

working like mine, only faster. "You still don't have a surname."

"You don't happen to remember Eddie's surname, do you, Mrs Stanley?" I asked, keeping my fingers crossed under the metal and Formica table.

"No, sorry, dear, I never did know that. Another biscuit?"

"No, thanks, we've got to meet some friends and go to the circus," said Seb, checking his watch. "And we're kind of late for them as it is."

"Thank you very much for talking to us," I said, remembering my manners as I stood up to go.

"Well, I only hope I helped a little!" Mrs Stanley smiled.

Had she helped? Or made things seem *more* impossible in a way?

I dunno.

I felt like I was in a real-life game of snakes and ladders, and after clambering up a couple of ladders, I was now slithering down one mighty big snake. . .

Chapter 15

Oops, I don't seem able to breathe...

"*What?*" Neisha asked, wrinkling her nose as if I'd just said the most ridiculous thing she'd ever heard.

How to make a girl feel stupid. . .

"The M-Mystic Marzipans," I said, my words backing up in my mouth and tripping over themselves to get out.

I wish I hadn't started this story. The Mystic Marzipans were a husband-and-wife clown team who'd rented the house opposite our cottage while they worked in Portbay. Their shows were corny but cute, a bit like their clown outfits. I'd only mentioned them because a) we were here in the big circus tent, waiting for the show to begin, and b) I was nervously trying to fill what felt like a giant-sized awkward silence.

The silence started long before me and Seb were even within talking distance of Frankie and the girls. You'd have had to be brain-dead or from another planet not to read the body language as we'd hurried over to meet them at the fancy old fountain in Victoria Park.

Had Seb spotted the bad vibes radiating my way? Did girl-on-girl bad vibes actually register on boys' radars? I wasn't so sure. . .

"It was so f-funny when TJ had a go on their unicycle!" I ploughed on, wishing I knew how to stop, and wishing the show would just start.

"A *what*?" Lauren asked, doing the same nose-wrinkling thing that Neisha did.

Eleni and Parminder were just staring at me. Frankie – sitting in the row behind the rest of us – didn't seem to be aware that I was even talking, she was so wrapped around Seb, smiling and chatting with him non-stop.

"A u-unicycle. Like a bike with one—"

A burst of laughter from all the little kids in the audience made me turn round to see what was happening. There'd been no announcements and the lights weren't down. . .

Aha – it was a clown running around the ring at high speed, as a bit of pre-show fun to get everyone going.

I sat properly round on my ringside bench, and tried to smile and pretend I was in the mood for fun.

But no amount of goofing around with buckets full of what looked like ominously green gloop was going to cheer me up today.

"You?" the clown was mouthing at a five-year-old girl, pointing to her, and then motioning for her to follow him and come stand in the middle of the ring. He whispered into her ear and she whispered back.

"Everyone please cheer for Sara!" he said, suddenly producing a microphone from his comedy-huge pocket.

I half-heartedly watched as he did the same thing to a couple of grinning little boys ("Darren!", "Mateo!"), who knew that they were about to be part of some trick that might or might not see them getting glooped.

The roared laughter of the crowds, the eyeball-frazzling brightness of the colours in the big top – my head was suddenly pounding madly. I'd have given anything to be instantly transported to the prom in Portbay, to feel the cool blue metal of the railings on my hands and the sea breeze on my flushed skin.

Then something Neisha was doing suddenly caught my attention: she seemed to be staring above, or just behind my head.

Oh – why had she slapped her hands over her mouth?

I swivelled round to catch sight of Frankie very exaggeratedly pointing her finger down towards the top of my head, trying – I realized with dread – to draw the clown's attention to me.

She didn't see me looking up at her; she was too busy grinning. Grinning at the clown who was now standing in front of me, I saw, as I spun round in my seat. His huge, painted-on red smile and nose were uncomfortably close.

"Come!" I heard him say, waving me to get up and join his other victims.

The laughter booming all around felt like it was pressing into me, squashing all the air out of my lungs.

As I struggled to draw breath, a zillion thoughts darted around in a high-speed panic.

Why is Frankie doing this? She's never done anything like this before! What's changed? Is it payback for spending time with her boyfriend? She knows how shy I get and how this is going to make me feel!

The clown loomed a step nearer. In the blaring muddle of laughter and noise I could just make out what he was saying.

"Tell me your name!"

The black microphone was the size of a fist, and threateningly close.

Would the crowds laugh even more as I stammered "S-S-Stella" into the mike, or go silent, all embarrassed for me?

Well, it wasn't going to happen.

I frantically felt around with shaking hands for my bag, and then ran. . .

Birds chirped. A Rasta guy cycled by, some mellow reggae station wafting out of a crummy little radio taped to his handlebars. Behind me, in a nursery that backed on to the park, two tiny kids were squabbling over whose turn it was to ride on the Bob the Builder trike.

"S'mine!"

"No! S'mine!"

"Noooooooo!"

"Yesssssssss!"

"Noooooooo!"

"*Wahhhhhhhhhhh!*"

The birdsong, the passing drift of reggae, the kiddy punch-up . . . it all sounded soothing to me. I think I'd found myself half-stumbling, half-hurrying to this particular bench just because I saw the children playing in that jumbled, happy way that my little brothers did.

And it was far enough from the circus tent to feel I could breathe again. The sound of the grating circus music was being blown in the opposite direction too, thanks to the blustery, storm's-coming wind that had blown out of nowhere.

Why's everything got so bad between me and Frankie and the girls? I fretted, staring up at a sky packed with racing, grey rain clouds. *I haven't flirted with Seb, I don't fancy him. But how come he's acting like more of a friend than my mates are?*

A sudden thought jagged into my head – he wouldn't follow me out here, would he? That would make things about ten zillion times worse. . .

I dropped my gaze, and sure enough saw a figure coming towards me. Thank goodness it was Parminder.

"You OK?" she called out, running over, holding her jacket closed against the wind.

"No," I said, smiling a wobbly smile at her.

She sat herself down beside me on the old, ornate park bench, which must have seen who-knows-how-many conversations take place on it over the last hundred years or so.

"That was a bit mean of Frankie," she conceded, tucking her long, black hair behind her ears as the wind tried to play with it.

"Yep," I agreed, nervously tucking my hands between my knees.

"But you have to see it from her point of view too. . ."

"What *is* her point of view?" I asked, genuinely, *desperately* wanting to know.

"Well, the whole thing with you and Seb, of course."

I felt like screaming. Not just a *scream* scream, but a howling yell of "I DO **NOT** FANCY SEB!!!!!" But screaming wasn't really me, and I didn't trust myself not to stammer at very loud volume.

"Parminder – I don't know what to do!" I groaned instead. "I mean, I really like Seb, but I absolutely *don't* fancy him, and I can't figure out how to get anyone to believe me!!"

Parminder blinked her dark eyelashes slowly and thoughtfully at me.

"Don't you get it, Stella?" she said. "Frankie thinks Seb fancies *you*!"

Boooooffff. . .

I felt like I'd been hit in the chest with one of Frankie's pillows.

"But why would she think *that*? Is it just because he's been helping me try and find out stuff about my grandparents?"

"Well, yeah." Parminder shrugged. "But it's more than that – it's the way he makes straight for you, every time he's been around lately. And Frankie says he never shuts up about you and your search thing."

I took a second to think about it. Seb following me to the café yesterday; Seb phoning Frankie and asking to be passed straight on to me; Seb breaking away from Frankie's hug that day at Camden Lock Market, right before the weird mirror moment.

I could totally see why Frankie might see things the way she did. But there was just one thing, and I didn't know quite how to put it in words that made any sense. It's just that when he looked at me, there was no . . . well . . . *wow* coming out of his eyes, like there was when I saw him spinning Frankie round at the play park.

A few seconds ago, I didn't know how I could convince Frankie and my friends that I didn't fancy Seb. Now I didn't know how to convince them that he absolutely didn't fancy *me*.

I let my head drop wearily back and stared at the clouds, trying to figure if they were blowing in the direction of Portbay.

"Stel?" Parminder mumbled, interrupting my muddled misery.

I dropped my head back down and turned to see her nodding at the top wooden panel of the bench.

Her arm, resting along the back of the bench, cast a shadow at first, and I couldn't make out the carved graffiti she seemed to be transfixed by.

"*For –*" read the first word, as I leant closer.

Only it wasn't the whole word.

"*Forever,*" that was it.

"It's them, isn't it?" said Parminder, voice hushed.

I let my finger run over all the words, hardly able to believe what I was seeing.

"*Forever and Ever and Evie, ♡ Eddie.*"

For the second time in the last ten minutes, I couldn't quite manage to breathe. . .

Chapter 16

Trapped in a fug of bad feeling

The capsule glided slowly upwards.

A couple started snogging, ignoring the view of London spreading out mesmerizingly below us.

A family of tourists from somewhere I couldn't work out pointed to the Houses of Parliament and said, "Buckingham Palace!!" in the middle of their complicated sounding language.

A man who suddenly realized he didn't like heights was sitting on the wooden bench in the middle of the pod with his head in his hands, groaning quietly, while his wife rubbed his back and muttered about how it was "supposed to be a treat, so he could at least try and promise not to be sick".

The London Eye: the most amazing structure you could see close up, even if it does look like the wheel of a giant space bicycle. Teetering over the river Thames and its famous bridges, you can see Alexandra Palace way to the north (where the first ever TV broadcasts came from) and Crystal Palace way to the south (where the once amazing giant glass building stood, showing off the wonders of the world a hundred-and-something years ago). You can see the dome of St Paul's Cathedral, Nelson's column, the BT Tower and the skyscrapers of Canary Wharf. You can see royal history in the distance at the Tower of London, and closer up, at Buckingham Palace (the real one, not the one that had been mistaken for the Houses of Parliament by the tourists).

I'd been here before, but I'd never enjoyed it less.

"Cashew?" I offered Frankie, who shook her head and pretended to be fascinated by the sight of a train trundling into Charing Cross on a bridge far below.

So much for Auntie V's last night treat: a ride on the Eye for me and Frankie (Auntie V was waiting down below, due to her vertigo) before she whisked us off to the opening night of a new musical that she'd had to pull serious strings to get tickets for.

And so much for hoping that I could maybe work things out with Frankie tonight.

This afternoon (this *freaky* afternoon), Parminder had left me sitting on the park bench, studying Eddie's love message in stunned silence, and promised to help me out. "I'll say you had a migraine," she told me, giving me an excuse not to go back to the circus. "And I'll try and talk to Frankie on her own. If I can't –" and I know Parminder probably couldn't, what with Frankie wrapping herself around Seb like a good luck charm warding off evil, "– I'll tell her that you and your Auntie V will come by for her at six o'clock. Is that right?"

It was. And when we stopped in a black cab outside Aunt Esme's flat, I knew for sure that Parminder *hadn't* been able to have that talk-on-her-own with Frankie. 'Cause Frankie had come out looking great – in a vivid green halterneck and low-slung combats – but had hardly looked my way, talking instead to Auntie V, and staring out of the window once the cab started driving off.

"You two go up on your own," Auntie V had said, handing us both our London Eye tickets when we got to the South Bank. "I can't go on – not with my head for heights!"

And now here we were, me and my supposed best friend, stuck in a big glass pod with a few foreign, snogging and potentially barfing strangers.

I fiddled with the sharp-edged, star-shaped

diamanté hairclips in my curl-fest of hair and tried again.

"Or what about . . . yogurt raisins?" I asked, searching in the treat bag that Auntie V had sorted out for us.

"Nah," said Frankie, gazing blankly down at the weaving lights of traffic below.

I didn't know quite what to do. Already, I was aching to pack it all in, and ask Auntie V to take us home as soon as this stupid capsule thing landed – but that wouldn't be for another twenty-five minutes anyway, till this giant space bike wheel inched its way round.

Twenty-five minutes trapped in a fug of bad feeling . . . how was I going to stop myself from going mad?

"CAAAAWWWWW!" a big-footed, cross-eyed seagull suddenly croaked outside of the capsule. (Everyone in the capsule could only imagine the sound, thanks to the double/triple/space-age glazing of the cigar-shaped units.)

I had an instant zap of déjà vu. Cut to three months earlier, my first week in Portbay, the last night of Frankie's visit, the two of us trapped at the top of a jammed Ferris wheel at the fair on the prom, swaying in the warm night air. The swaying was stressing Frankie out, and she got a whole lot *more* stressed when a seagull casually landed on the back of our rocking gondola.

"Hey, look!" I gently nudged Frankie, ready to point out the flapping, slightly familiar-looking seagull outside our pod. "D'you remember that night in Portbay, when—"

"Don't you *ever* shut up about Portbay?" Frankie rounded on me, lifting an angry face up to meet mine.

"W-wh-*what*?" I stammered.

Whether I wanted it or not (I didn't) it seemed like a full-scale argument was on the way. I hated arguing at the best of times, but having one while stuck on a slow-moving capsule with a bunch of strangers felt like a *very* bad idea.

"It's always Portbay *this*, and Portbay *that*," she imitated me barbedly. "I don't know why you ever *bothered* to come back to London in the first place!"

"To see *you* and the other girls, of course!" I tried to defend myself, aware that everyone was now staring, even the ones who were pretending they weren't.

"Yeah, *right!*"

I suddenly wished I could text my smart-mouthed friends like TJ or Rachel or Tilda for a great, cutting-edge response, but it would take too long to text, and all the while Frankie would be scowling menacingly at me.

"Yes, *right*!" I insisted uselessly.

"Ha!"

Our loud bickering was obviously enough to crush the romantic moment for the snogging couple, who broke off from each other to join in the general staring.

"So why have you spent the last week going on and on and *on* about your mates there? It's either that, or you're off sniggering over their texts without telling us what they're about!"

Was she talking about the texts I got on Wednesday, when we were all in TopShop?

"But it was just stuff – nothing important!"

I could hardly tell her that I'd been moaning to TJ and Rachel and everyone about the dull time I was having right then.

"What, because maybe you were having a *laugh* with them about me and the girls?!"

Yikes, had she somehow seen what I was texting after all?

"Yeah, you can't deny it, can you?" smirked Frankie. "All this week, you've been reading texts from them, and then smiling and just shoving your phone away when any of us ask what they've said!"

So it *wasn't* just Wednesday she was talking about. That should've made me feel relieved, but somehow it didn't. 'Cause somehow I'd given the impression that I was more interested in my Portbay mates, and my London mates had got it into their heads that I was talking about them behind their backs!

"B-but that's not . . . I mean, I wasn't. . ."

"Yeah, *yeah*," Frankie said in a mocking voice, crossing her arms defensively across her chest. "*Sure* you weren't taking the mickey out of us. Just like you *haven't* spent the whole time dissing London –"

Had I? Had I moaned about London? Maybe I had; I vaguely remembered muttering about how much litter there was the day we went to Camden Lock Market, and how crowded central London felt the day we all went shopping. But had I really moaned that much?

"– just like you *haven't* acted like the publicity officer for the Portbay Tourist Office, the amount you go on about it –"

Did I go on about Portbay all the time? If I had, it was only because I thought the girls might be interested in my new home town, and my new life.

"– and just like you have *no* idea Seb has a thing for you!!"

166

Oops.

I felt like I'd just been drenched in a gungey, bucket-load of sarcasm.

Like most super-confident girls, Frankie was a hundred times better at arguing than me, so how could I stand up for myself? How could I say that I wasn't bitching with my Portbay mates, that I *didn't* mean to diss London, that I hadn't meant to be boring about Portbay, that Seb really, REALLY didn't fancy me?

"You're wrong," I tried to say as forcefully as I could.

"About what, exactly?" Frankie growled.

I gulped. And begged myself not to stammer.

"Seb – he doesn't like me . . . not like *that*. He's just trying to be kind."

"Oh, yeah?" said Frankie, loudly enough for the might-be-sick guy to look up from his seat on the bench now. "Well, *I* don't think that's true, which is why I *chucked* him tonight, right before you came round!"

"You what?!"

The foreign family with the indistinguishable language and the lousy identification skills could obviously understand English better than I had expected, from the way they had all tilted their eyes and ears in our direction.

"Well, what did you expect me to do?" Frankie spat out. "*I* don't need a boyfriend who tells me off like I'm some little kid, and then takes sides with someone else!"

And *I* was that someone else, I supposed.

"Why did he tell you off?" I asked, trying to think which chunk of Frankie's lairyness might have got to him. It just dawned on me what it was, when she started to speak (OK, yell) at me again.

"He said I wasn't being very '*nice*' to you this afternoon, when I tried to get the clown to get you up!"

There it was again: that sarcasm overload.

"But you *weren't* being very nice!" I said, knowing it sounded lame, but too stunned to do any better.

"Yeah? Well, it's not very nice having a boyfriend who drools over your best mate, and a best mate who pretends not to notice!"

Frankie was so wrong it made my head hurt.

I *had* to sort this out. Ideas raced round my mind at high speed, before tripping themselves up by being too useless.

Then I saw a glint of silver metal poking out of Frankie's jeans pocket. And grabbed it fast.

"Stella! What are you playing at?! Give me that back!!" Frankie ordered.

"Nope," I said, quickly stepping backwards away from her, and pressing the "on" key on the mobile I'd just pinched from her.

The phone burst into life, but I ignored the shrill of the many messages Seb had left her, and which she'd kept her phone switched off to avoid.

Flip-flip-flip went my fingers, as I quickly accessed the address book.

"You've got to give him a chance to explain it's not true," I told her, swirling around so the phone was out of her reach.

(Flip, flip, flip; I wished "S" didn't come so far down on the phone book list. . .)

"Stella!! I said *give* it to me!"

As Frankie lunged, I grabbed her outstretched arm. The whole of the other pod passengers were staring openly now, probably anticipating a cat-fight any second.

But I knew there wouldn't be, not if Seb picked up his phone right now.

"Just hold on," I said, gripping pretty firmly on to Frankie's wrist. "If I *prove* to you that you got it wrong about Seb, then you've got to understand you got the rest of that stuff kind of wrong too!"

Frankie's big brown eyes stared into mine, but not in any fierce way any more, like she was aiming to tear lumps of honey-coloured hair out or anything. It was more a stare of total confusion. I knew right then that she'd been on as much of a mood rollercoaster as I had the past few days. In her own way, she'd been just as muddled and oversensitive as I had. And we'd been friends for so long that we just *had* to sort this thing out. . .

"God, Frankie!" Seb's voice said into my ear, as he assumed he'd recognized who was calling. "Why'd you switch your phone off? I've been calling and calling. . ." His voice sounded different, like he was upset and confused and trying really hard not to show it.

Pulling the mobile away from my face for a second, I clicked the speakerphone key.

"Hi, Seb – it's not Frankie, it's Stella. I'm just borrowing her phone, that's all," I replied, gazing at Frankie – who looked even *more* furious. Was she going to call out to him? She didn't; keen, I supposed, to stay quiet (a once-in-a-lifetime experience) and see what he had to say for himself.

"Oh. Um, hi, Stella!" Seb replied, sounding bewildered. "Are you OK? Is your migraine better?"

"Yeah, it's fine," I answered Seb quickly. "Listen, I just wanted to check something with you."

My heart was thundering in my chest, not just because his answer could ruin a practically life-long friendship, but because everyone in the pod had now given up on the stunning, unique vista of London and were now brazenly listening in.

"Yeah? What's that?" his voice boomed out of the speakerphone.

Frankie's lips were pressed tightly together, but her chest was heaving like some historical heroine in a corset, instead of a funky London girl in a green halter-neck top.

"I just wanted to ask. . ."

A rush of embarrassment flooded over me, as if every vein was being pumped full of warm bathwater.

". . .did Frankie tell you that I used to fancy you?"

I swear I heard a group gasp from everyone in the pod. But it suddenly, amazingly didn't bother me; I was just thrilling to the fact that I'd said something so cringeworthy *without stammering*.

"I, uh . . . yeah. She did."

Keep going, keep going, I told myself, my whole being curling up with the mortification of it all

"Is that why you've been so nice to me? I mean, 'cause you felt a bit sorry for me or something?"

"Well, yeah. I mean, I just thought it must be really . . . y'know, hard, or uncomfortable for you or whatever. I just thought it'd make it a little easier, if I was friendly and showed you I wasn't, uh, freaked by it."

Ahhhh . . . *exactly* what I wanted to hear.

"Listen, Stella, you don't *still* . . . y'know. . ."

Eeek!

"*No!* I don't! Not at all!" I assured him quickly, without using the dreaded "f" word.

I kept my gaze on Frankie – seeing what she made of all this – but her lips were still pressed together in the same iron lock, giving nothing away about what was churning around behind those dark eyes.

"It's just . . . don't get me wrong, Stella," Seb carried on, "I really like you, but. . ."

At that beautiful sounding "but" I felt a bit weak in the knee department. Maybe some of the watching pod passengers thought I was about to keel over from total rejection instead of blissed-out relief.

". . .just as a friend. I mean, I'm really into all this stuff you're doing, trying to find your grandad and everything. It's just, well, I'm sitting at my computer right now, looking for sites about Somalia. So that's all, really. I mean – I mean,

172

that's OK with you, right? I don't want to hurt your feelings or anything!"

"It's *more* than OK – it's brilliant," I said, smiling hopefully at Frankie.

But instead of smiling back, Frankie just looked a bit tearful and turned away, pretending to gaze out at the night-time sky.

"Oh. . ." I heard Seb say, obviously confused at my slightly delirious response to his knock-back.

"It's fine, Seb, honest," I told him, hoping to make it clear that I wasn't about to throw myself off the Tower of London, thanks to a bad case of unrequited love. "I know how you feel about Frankie."

"Yeah, well, I love her and everything, Stella. . ."

I saw Frankie close her eyes, and lean her forehead against the cool glass of the pod.

She stayed that way for the next twenty minutes, while I perched on the bench in the middle of the pod (beside the barfing man).

I watched her and watched her, till the cycle of the Eye took us back down to earth. . .

Chapter 17

Secrets and guilt and promises

Pride and Prejudice by Jane Austen.

I haven't read the book, but I saw the DVD that was out a few years ago, starring Keira Knightley, and it was pretty good, if you're into old-fashioned romance stuff, with girls dressed in floaty frocks who say stuff like "Oh, Mama!" at regular intervals.

Before this latest version of *Pride and Prejudice* started tonight, Auntie V had explained to me and Frankie that there had been *blah-de-blah* amount of editions published of the book since it was first in bookshops back in 18-*blah-de-blah*, and that there had been *blah-de-blah* amount of TV and film versions of it – including a Bollywood movie – over the last few decades.

Sorry for all the vague *blah-de-blah*s. But I was so fazed by the fight with Frankie, the phone call to Seb, and the frosty silence between me and my supposed best friend ever since that I hadn't been completely concentrating on what Auntie V had said. That includes from the time that she met us off the London Eye, during the black cab journey over to the theatre, till we were sitting in our seats and gazing blankly at the programmes she'd bought us.

But then again, maybe one thing *did* manage to wriggle its way into my overstretched, bruised-with-emotion brain. With so many reprinted books, with so many TV and film productions, did the world *really* need to see another variation of *Pride and Prejudice?*

Specially a *musical* one, set in *space?*

"*I look at yoooo and the galaxy has no end, everyone is my friend!*" sang a man on the stage, overacting badly in a tight spacesuit that looked a bit *too* tight all over. It was a wonder Darcy the hunky rocketship captain wasn't singing soprano.

Now it was the turn of the beautiful, three-eyed alien heroine Lizzie.

"*I gazed at yoooo and both my hearts missed a beat, even though –*"

"*– you've got smelly feet!*" Frankie leant over and whisper-sang in my ear.

It was weird. After sitting frostily beside each other for the whole of this awful show so far, after

175

icily ignoring each other and talking only to Auntie V over ice cream at the intermission, just that sudden slice of silliness somehow cut through the horrible murk of misunderstandings, crossed wires and bad feelings that had enveloped me and Frankie.

Now that this horror of a show was creaking towards its finale, one cheeky line whispered from Frankie had us both creasing and crumpling, struggling to giggle hysterically in the quietest way possible as we clung on to each other.

And then as an inexplicable barrage of applause signalled the end of the show, I heard something I hadn't expected to hear. At all.

"I'm sorry," Frankie whispered in my ear, squeezing my hand really tight. "I think I got some stuff wrong. . ."

"Me too," I whispered back, feeling Frankie's many tiny plaits tickle my nose.

And then we sat up straighter and looked at each other, as if we were both trying to forget the last week and remember why we'd liked each other for all those years.

Meanwhile, the audience around us continued to clap and cheer for the seriously awful show they'd just witnessed.

Although I kind of liked to imagine all that

clapping and cheering was for me and Frankie, in honour of us making up. . .

"Stella, this had better just be a four-tissue situation, because I've run out!" said Auntie V, hugging me tight in the back of the black cab home, and showing me the empty pack of what had once been a full, handbag-sized tissue pack in her hand.

"I think so," I told her, now that my swollen eyes and puffy nose had finally stopped streaming.

It had been three minutes since we'd dropped off Frankie at her Kentish Town flat and me and Frankie had hugged each other goodbye like there'd be no tomorrow (and there wouldn't be, because I was heading back to Portbay in the morning).

After giving us enough time for hugs and tears and byes and sorrys, Auntie V – probably watching the meter ticking at the front of the black cab – had gently called an end to proceedings and cuddled me close as the cab sped off into the night, towards Highgate.

The last I saw of Frankie, she was pulling her mobile out, ready to call Seb, I bet, and tell him he was forgiven (well, she'd used up all tonight's sorrys on *me*).

"So, Stella my little star, that was a very strange night, wasn't it?"

If I'd been in a flippant mood, which I absolutely wasn't, I might have joked that the whole idea of *Pride and Prejudice* as a musical set in space was more than strange, it was *insane*.

But I knew Auntie V wasn't talking about that.

"Do you want to tell me what was going on?" she prompted me.

"It's just been really weird," I sniffled into the last, sopping wet tissue that I had. (The other three – even more sopping wet – were on the floor of the black cab.)

"Weird how?"

"I've just felt . . . sort of like an outsider or something," I said, realizing I'd had a similar sort of conversation with Aunt Esme last night, in her kitchen.

(Aunt Esme – I hadn't said bye! Frankie and me had been too wound up in each other when the cab had stopped to remember that Aunt Esme would've been expecting a goodbye bear hug from me too!)

"What, you mean you feel an outsider being back in London?" asked Auntie V.

"A little bit, I suppose. But it's more my friends: it's like I always thought I knew them and they knew me, but then this week they've sometimes acted as if they don't get me at *all*. Specially Frankie. Till last thing tonight, I mean!"

"Well, you've probably changed more than you realize, Stella!"

"*That* doesn't sound good," I mumbled.

"Don't be silly! Change is fine!" said Auntie V, hugging me closer and wiping away the hairs sticking to my clammy forehead. "You've just got to realize it might never be the same with your London friends."

I must have jerked or looked a bit scared or something, because Auntie V immediately qualified what she was trying to say.

"Not the same day-to-day, I mean. But that's just because you're not *with* them, day-to-day, any more! You've got to remember that your *new* day-to-day friends are back in Portbay. As for Frankie Etc., you can still be good mates with them all, but just not in exactly the same *way* as before. Do you know what I mean?"

"I think so." I nodded, remembering with a knot of sadness that I hadn't said goodbye to Parminder and the others either, since I'd left Victoria Park while they were all still at the circus.

"I just think all of you – your expectations of

each other, and how easily you thought you'd all slot back together – they were just too high."

"Maybe," I murmured, feeling soothed by her warm but matter-of-fact words, and by the hypnotic stream of London shop lights whirling by as we drove on in the night.

"And they maybe just need to get used to the fact that in the place of their old shy friend they've got a new, pretty confident one!"

I smiled wryly at Auntie V's compliment.

"I haven't felt *that* confident this week . . . my stammer's come back a bit."

"Hmm. Have you been feeling like you've taken a step back?"

Yes – she was right, exactly right, I *did* feel like I'd taken a step back. A step back to the more insecure version of me.

And no – that wasn't really the reason I'd often been quiet when I'd been hanging out with her at the flat.

"It's just . . . there's this thing. . ." I found myself saying, realizing that I was on the verge of spilling my secret. Was it too late to backtrack?

"Don't tell me: you've been planning a bank raid!" Auntie V joked, tricking me into an unexpected giggle.

"No!" I smiled at her. "I've just been . . . well,

it's just that I've been on a kind of mission, trying to find out something – *anything* – about my Grandad Eddie."

"How interesting," said Auntie V, in a genuinely intrigued voice. "But why haven't you said?"

"I've been to Hackney a couple of times, to see the house where Evie – my Nana Jones – used to live, and to the park where the fairground was, the place where Eddie and Evie met up."

"When did you go to Hackney?" said Auntie V, in a more measured voice now. (Was she going to be angry with me, for going so far without telling her?)

"On Monday, with Frankie and her boyfriend Seb."

"When you said you were just going to be hanging around hers all day?"

(Auntie V's arm was still around my shoulders – I hoped that was a good sign.)

"Yep. And today – with all the girls."

"But I thought you told me you were going to a circus with them, over at Highbury Fields?"

"We *did* go to the circus, only it was in Victoria Park, not Highbury Fields."

"And you fibbed to me *why*, exactly?"

(She didn't sound thrilled, but she didn't sound furious either.)

181

"You'd have had to tell Mum that I wanted to go there, and she'd have thought it was too far for me to travel, even if I was with my friends."

"Yes, you're probably right there."

"And I didn't want her to know I was looking for clues about Grandad Eddie, or stuff about Evie, in case it upset her, because she's been a bit funny about it lately."

"Maybe because she's grown up all her life in London, and moving to Portbay severed her last ties with her parents, even if they're not alive any more."

Wow.

I'd never thought of it like that; it wasn't just *me* who'd had to leave the place I'd grown up in; in her own adult way, Mum had gone through exactly the same thing as me.

We sat in silence for a second, as the taxi rumbled on, and I took on board what Auntie V had just said. Then an important point pinged into my head.

"Aren't you going to tell me off?" I asked, looking around at her, at the halo of brightness gleaming from her hair as the street lights flickered by.

"What's the point?" she said, with a shrug of the cream pashmina draped over her shoulders.

"I know I should probably have a rant at you, but I think you've managed to make yourself miserable enough with guilt over this, haven't you? That's why you've been so quiet, isn't it?"

"Um, yes . . . I guess so."

"Well, there you go. And it's your last night, so I really don't want to spoil it by having to turn all school teacher-y and lecturing you."

"Thank you," I whispered, in a teeny-tiny voice.

"Just promise you won't do it again. Secretly running halfway across London to investigate missing grandparents, I mean."

She'd got me grinning again, with her flippant remark.

"I promise," I told her, very, *very* glad all of a sudden that moving to Portbay had changed our relationship so completely and so brilliantly.

"So secrets and guilt and promises aside," said Auntie V, right after she'd directed the driver to turn off the main road, "was it mission impossible? Or did you manage to find out anything new about your grandfather?"

"Only two things; I met an old neighbour of Evie's family, who said she'd chatted to him and he was really nice."

"Well, *that's* something," said Auntie V positively,

nodding her head so that her sharp blonde bob bobbed.

"And today," I began to say, my heart surging at the memory, "I found an old carving on a bench in Victoria Park. It said, 'Forever and Ever and Evie, ♡ Eddie'!"

"Really?!" Auntie V's perfectly plucked eyebrows shot up her forehead.

"Yeah, really! I just wished I had a camera with me. . ."

"Left here, please," Auntie V suddenly instructed the driver, as we approached the street where she lived. "Well, that's pretty remarkable, Stella, don't you think?"

"Absolutely! But I wish I could've found out more. If I'd just managed to get a second name for him, maybe. . ."

"Just here, thanks!" Auntie V called out to the driver, taking her arm away and rifling in her bag for her purse.

I opened up the heavy cab door, bounded out and held it open for her.

"The thing is, Stella," she said, as she elegantly slithered one long leg out, "some stories never tie up all the loose ends. Real life isn't like the plot of musicals, with neat beginnings, middles and ends."

"Or rotten songs," I nearly joked, till I

184

remembered how many strings Auntie V had said she'd pulled to get tickets for the dreadful show tonight.

"So don't be too disappointed," she continued, handing the driver some money. "Just try and enjoy the mystery and romance of Eddie and Evie, and be glad you accidentally stumbled on something so special!"

Auntie V was right in most of what she said – just not the part about me accidentally stumbling on the carved graffiti. Like most important, special and magical things that had happened to me since I'd moved to Portbay, I didn't think there was anything accidental about it at all.

"And *next* time you come to visit," said Auntie V, linking her arm into mine, "maybe you and I can pay a non-secret visit to Victoria Park together, and take a camera this time?"

I leant into Auntie V, grateful to have an auntie as cool, funny and kind as her.

Even if she *did* have dubious taste in stage shows. . .

Chapter 18

Banana fritters and much-missed friends. . .

I was humming and hawing over which magazine to get for the train journey home, when a long, slender arm stretched across my eyeline and scooped up four of the covers I was gazing at.

"Hey, it's a long journey, you might get bored," Auntie V shrugged, as she sashayed over towards the pay desk.

She'd already bought me a whole bag of posh, picnic-y nibbles from M&S.

"Thank you," I said, as we headed out of WHSmith's and back on to the concourse at Paddington Station.

"Don't be *too* grateful – *you're* carrying this stuff!" she said, all mock bossy, as she handed me the plastic bags of nibbles and mags.

But I *was* grateful to her, and not just 'cause of the stuff she was buying me. I was grateful to her for inviting me to London in the first place, and grateful for her wise words and lack of telling-off last night. And I was very grateful to her for the extra-special, last-minute surprise she'd landed on me this morning. . .

"Thought I'd spoil you with some breakfast in bed," she'd said, holding the pale wood-and-white tray as I blinked myself awake and sat myself up.

Orange juice and warm croissants with jam . . . plus (and *this* was the extra-special, last-minute surprise) my photo of Eddie and Evie, framed in a plain, thick band of antique silver.

I'd shown her the photo, the love letter and the fan last night, after we got back to her flat. I guess I'd left them sitting on the coffee table when I'd finally flopped off to bed, exhausted by the day.

"It's just some old frame I wasn't using," Auntie V had said casually, as I picked up the photo and gazed at it. "There's no point letting something like that get all dog-eared, is there?"

I loved the way Auntie V hid her heart of gold under a veneer of brashness. And I loved the way she now click-clacked importantly across the concourse – and then stopped by the silliest of stalls.

"What are we doing?" I asked, grinning at the sight of my elegant Auntie V browsing along

187

shelves of Paddington Bear mugs, key rings and soft toys.

"Let me see, Stella . . . you've been so busy hanging out and falling out with your friends, not to mention going on time-consuming secret missions, that I'm guessing you've completely forgotten to buy any presents for your little brothers."

"Oh. . ." I mumbled, realizing she was very definitely right.

"We'll take this and this," Auntie V said to the girl on the stall, pointing to two eggcups with matching spoons, decorated with the famous toy bear from Paddington (via Peru).

I held my carrier bag open, ready for her to drop in my last-minute gifts when I heard a terrible noise. Everyone else hovering around the concourse heard the terrible noise too, and looked round in alarm.

The yelling and screeching, the bundle of people hurtling from the tube station entrance . . . had something awful happened down there?!

Panic over – my eyes and ears suddenly tuned in.

The people were mostly teenage girls, and they were hurtling towards this stall.

And in amongst their excitable screeches and

yells, I could hear one specific word: "STELLAAAAAAAAA!!!"

One page of *Mizz* and half a banana fritter.

That was as much as I'd managed to read and eat before I fell asleep on the train, worn out from my rollercoaster ride of a week.

And my dreams were like a replay of everything that had happened, a jumble of sleepovers and circuses, changing rooms and cemeteries, discoveries and disappointments, museums and more-than-plenty of misunderstandings.

Then there was a rerun of what had happened back at the station earlier; the total shock and fantastic surprise of seeing Frankie and all of my girlfriends bundling towards me, doing the whole bursting-my-eardrums-with-squealing-and-ribs-with-hugs thing that I'd sort of imagined when I'd first arrived at Paddington a week ago. (Well, better late than never, I guess.)

"The tube stopped for *ages* in a tunnel!" Neisha had gabbled.

"We didn't think we'd get here in time!"; "We thought we'd miss you!"; "We couldn't let you go without saying bye!" came a babble of conversation from the other girls.

"It's cool between us, yeah?" Frankie had said in a voice spookily quiet and shy for her.

Before I'd got the chance to say yes of *course*, an out-of-breath Aunt Esme broke through the girl gaggle to squash me in her own farewell hug.

"Take these for the train," she'd said, when she finally let me go, handing me a plastic box of what I knew had to be banana fritters.

In my hazy dream state, I fast-forwarded to the moment I was waving at them all from the train, Auntie V and Aunt Esme standing side by side, looking like a human version of a toddler game of "Opposites" (except they both had matching tears in their eyes). Beside them, my girlfriends were waving so hard their hands were nearly a blur.

Then there was Frankie, running alongside of the moving train, blowing kiss after kiss after kiss, till speeding wheels took me away from her. . .

Ping! went my eyelids suddenly, as something woke me up.

I squidged upright in my seat, rubbing my face where it had gone numb from leaning up against the window, and glanced around to see what had jerked me out of my sleep rambles.

Bleep!

Not one message on my phone, not two messages, but five, all from my much-missed Portbay mates.

Welcome home!! If you're there, I mean!! (From Megan, who always overdosed on exclamation marks.)

Am bored. Stuck helping Mum in her shop, so can't come meet you – boo! Have you bought present? Better have! (Rachel, who I suddenly realized was an awful lot like Auntie V.)

Are u back yet? Working at the café today – come c me? Will save u a muffin! (Amber, busy, but thinking of me.)

Fancy a walk 2 the headland this aft., & c what's happening in Sugar Bay? (Tilda, who'd loved Joseph's House as much as I did, though it took me a long time to find that out.)

Woof, woof, woof, woof, lick! (TJ, in the guise of Bob the dog.)

TJ (and Bob). . .

I'd been a hundred per cent sure that he (OK, *they*, since boy and dog were inseparable) would be there waiting for me at Portbay station, along with Mum and Dad and the twins.

TJ was, I realized, with a jolt to the heart, just as much my best friend as Frankie had ever been, and I couldn't *wait* to see him. . .

And – not counting Bob – what about my non-human buddy? Would Peaches be mooching casually around the station, wrapping his raggedy ginger tail round the base of the ticket machine?

He'd been in my thoughts already this morning. While I'd nibbled on my croissant in bed, I'd gazed up at the artily-menacing *Médée* poster and seen nothing but a few green leaves scattered on the rumpled robes of the heroine, just where those green cat's eyes had gleamed at me.

Had I imagined them all along, to keep me company?

I didn't have long to mull that over before a glimpse of an upcoming small station caught my eye. It was the station where I'd seen a familiar looking ginger cat curled up on a bench on the platform. Would it be there again? Adrenaline pumped through my veins as the train raced through, and ebbed straight away as I glimpsed nothing more than an empty bench.

Oh well, I murmured silently to myself, relaxing back in my seat when—

NEE NAH!!

The train whistle made me jerk to attention, as we swept over a level crossing, its red lights flashing and its white barriers down. In a snatched second, I noticed a couple of cars parked up and waiting, and a pedestrian leaning on the barrier, smiling and waving at the train. For the minutest of moments, I made eye contact with the pedestrian – an old lady – and automatically put my hand up to wave back.

She winked at me, I was sure. Just as sure as I was that she was dressed in an apple-green raincoat with a marshmallow-pink netted hat perched on her head.

I might not have found everything I wanted in London, but it didn't seem to matter now.

My heart soared; I was going home. . .

Chapter 19

Excuse me, but are you real?!

Sparkling sea, endless sand, ice-cream cones with Flakes and raspberry sauce.

There couldn't be a nicer way to spend Sunday morning with your friends.

Well, there could – take away the chilly October wind that was blasting an icing of sand on to our cones and it would have been pretty much perfect.

How TJ's little sister Ellie could bear paddling, I had no idea, but then five-year-olds have as much sense as not-very-clever starfish.

"I'm f-f-freezing!" grumbled Rachel, as strands of her long dark hair were blown into her ice-cream.

I smiled to myself, glad that the only person doing any stammering round here was my under-dressed friend.

"Here, wrap this around you!" said TJ, handing her a corner of the tartan travel rug I'd optimistically taken with me, thinking that we could all sit and lounge on the beach and catch up with each other. (Stand shivering on the beach and catch hypothermia together seemed more likely.)

"I'd rather get frostbite!" Rachel grimaced, stamping her feet to keep warm and ignoring the offer.

It was a style thing, as far as Rachel was concerned – she's worryingly obsessed with fashion, even if short skirts, bare legs and ballet pumps don't particularly work in a howling gale.

"You could hug Bob if you like! Go on!" TJ teased Rachel, shoving his hairy, happy dog towards her.

"No *thanks*!" said Rachel, rolling her eyes and swapping places with Tilda.

"He's only a dog! He's not poisonous!" Tilda told her off.

Tilda was wearing her usual outfit of leather jacket, tutu and stripy tights, but her mum had knitted her a pair of purple, fingerless gloves, I noticed – perfect for holding ice-creams on a cold day. And the jacket was perfect for keeping the chill off her pet rat, who peeked his head out of her inside pocket just long enough to sniff cautiously at the raspberry sauce he'd smelled wafting around.

"Did you *have* to bring Xenon out with you today?" Rachel frowned at Tilda. "If it hadn't been for your dumb rat, we could've gone and sat in the café, and at least been warm!"

"You've got a lead for Xenon, right?" TJ asked Tilda.

Tilda nodded, and gave Xenon (or Mr Noodles, as she called him when she thought we weren't listening) a stroke along his delicate, smooth head.

"Well, you could tie him up outside the Hot Pepper Jelly, alongside Bob!" TJ suggested. "They could keep each other company!"

"Yeah, and scare off anyone planning to come in and eat!" laughed Amber, her arms held tightly across the front of her denim jacket. (Underneath was her apron, T-shirt-and-cropped-jeans uniform, ready for her Sunday shift at the caff.)

"Well, d'you guys want to come back to mine?" Tilda offered.

Tilda's black-painted room was as cosy as a crypt, but at least it would be warm. Still, it wasn't an option for a couple of us.

"Can't – got to start work in fifteen minutes." Amber shrugged, vivid red strands of hair escaping from her loose plait.

"And I've got to be home in half an hour," I told

Tilda. "I'm going out with my parents and the boys this afternoon."

("Let's spend some proper family-time together, out of the house!" Mum had said this morning, after two hours spent cleaning up a spilt tin of paint that the twins had emptied over the kitchen floor.)

"OK, but I'm warning you – I may die if I don't get warm soon!" Rachel moaned.

"Then *wear* the rug!" TJ insisted, picking it up and holding it out towards her. "Look, I'll wrap it round you now!"

As TJ lurched towards her with an evil grin, Rachel squealed, "No way!" and took a few steps backwards, which was like a red rag to a bull as far as TJ was concerned.

"Nooooo!" yelped Rach, as TJ chased her zig-zagging across the sands, holding the rug up to catch her in.

"Well, *that'll* warm her up," said Tilda, stroking Xenon's inquisitive nose. "Don't know what *we're* going to do though."

"I know what Megan would say!" Amber suddenly smiled.

"What?" I asked, thinking of our faraway friend, the missing piece of the Portbay version of Stella Etc., as Auntie would've put it.

"Cartwheels!" said Amber, uncrossing her arms. "You up for it?"

I didn't need to be asked twice. Throwing what was left of my ice-cream to the wind, I starting thumping in wonky circles down the sands, towards the splashing surf and the equally splashing Ellie.

At one, brief, upside-down moment, I saw the podgy psycho seagull swoop down to grab the remnants of my cone, before flapping back up to the sky.

And then a familiar Portbay sound intruded on the seagull cawing and sea-swooshing sounds of the beach: an out-of-season coach, trundling along the prom, about to drop its party of OAP daytrippers at the Hot Pepper Jelly for tea and cakes.

So what would some of those old ladies and gents see, if they gazed down at the beach now? A girl in a tutu, stroking a rat and laughing at two other girls doing terrible, wobbly cartwheels, while a boy, a dog and rug chased a squealing girl into the sea, where she got unceremoniously soaked with splashes by a giggling little girl who seemed to mistake the bitter breeze for summer sunshine.

"Young people today," they'd probably tut. "Crazy, the lot of them."

And you know something? They'd be right, I'm very happy to say. . .

The café in Pavilion Park was packed, thanks to the even chillier wind blowing people in from their Sunday afternoon strolls.

Somewhere outside, forced to be oblivious to the cold, Dad was playing hide 'n' seek ('n' shriek) with my little brothers.

Safely inside, I hugged my hot chocolate, feeling so numb that I didn't notice how hot the mug was till it started to singe my hands.

"All right?" asked Mum, sitting next to me at the small round table by the window.

She wasn't asking if I was all right because of the singed hands, and I wasn't numb because of the cold. My numbness and her concern were both down to the fact that she'd just announced she knew.

As in *knew*.

It turned out that as soon as I was safely on the train yesterday, Auntie V had called Mum and told her . . . well, *everything*.

I'd thought about telling her, I just hadn't figured out how and when. Now I was just numb with surprise, since Mum was the one doing the telling, right here, right now.

"Are you annoyed with me?" I finally managed to say, sneaking a peek at her through my curtain of blown-about curls.

"Stella, honey," she sighed, brushing my hair back from my face as she spoke. "I'm not exactly thrilled at the idea of you jaunting around London without me or your Auntie V knowing. But I think your reasons for doing it were very sweet."

"But you're not upset?" I asked, checking that my secret mission hadn't set her off on her own rocky rollercoaster of emotions.

"Listen, I'm normally fine when I think about your nana, but it's just got to me lately – missing her, I suppose – because all the upheaval of moving here has been so tiring."

I looked longer into her face than I had done for ages; there did seem to be a few more lines around her brown eyes. And were there a few greys in amongst the dark hair that tumbled just past her shoulders?

"You *do* like it here, don't you?" I asked, suddenly hit with the notion that *she* might regret the life-switch that I now *loved*.

"Oh, absolutely!" she said genuinely. "Even though I'm tired it feels totally right to be—"

"Excuse me. . ." a woman's voice interrupted us.

"Would it be all right if my husband and I shared your table?"

"Of course!" Mum smiled up at the fifty-something-year-old lady, who was wearing a new-looking rain jacket, which is usually the uniform of the tourist round here. "Please help yourselves!"

The suspected tourist sat down, patting her ruffled blondy-grey hair flat after its buffeting from the wind.

"He's just up getting a cup of tea," the woman explained, nodding her head in the vague direction of the counter, and settling herself into a chair.

"Right," Mum replied politely, looking as if she was about to turn back to me and continue our conversation.

"Not much of a start to our holidays, this weather!" the woman chattered on, unzipping her jacket and making herself at home.

Uh-oh. I could tell she was going to be exactly like Mumsy Denise, on the train to London last week, one of those pleasant but determined people who aren't going to be put off having a chat by anything as unimportant as the other person's lack of interest in joining in.

"Um . . . so you're on holiday?" Mum was forced to ask.

"Yes!" The woman nodded. "Just came on the train from London yesterday!"

("Oooh!" muttered the coincidence monitor in my head.)

"Mmm!" Mum mumbled pleasantly, still hoping, I thought, that she might be able to slip away from this conversation.

(*Fat chance*, I thought silently, knowing better.)

"We're staying at the Sea View Holiday Park. The caravans up on the cliffs at the other end of the bay. Do you know it?"

"*I* do!" I blurted out, before Mum could reply. The caravan park was where Megan's family had stayed on holiday, and I'd been up there only yesterday afternoon with Tilda and TJ (and Bob), gazing down at the new holiday homes being built in Sugar Bay.

"You can ask my daughter *anything* about this town!" Mum laughed. "We only moved here a few months ago, but Stella's a real expert on the place!"

"Really!" the woman widened her blue eyes at me. "Well, *that's* very interesting! You might be able to save us a bit of time. My husband's very keen to find a place called Joseph's House. Do you know it?"

I think my mum took my stunned silence for shyness and jumped in.

"Well," she said, shooting me a quick look, "I'm afraid you're a little bit too late. Joseph's House burned down a few weeks ago."

"Oh!" The woman gave a little gasp, her lipsticked smile turning into a little circle of disappointment.

"It used to be in Sugar Bay, right where you're staying!" I burst in, finding my voice at last.

"What – you mean where all that building work is going on now?"

"Uh-huh," I said with a nod.

"Oh, that's a pity, a real pity," the woman said thoughtfully. "My husband had been really keen to see it. . ."

"Um, why?" I heard myself ask, hoping it didn't sound too rude.

"Well, since he took early retirement this year, he's busied himself trying to do his family tree. He's traced his family back to Barbados, and he thinks he may be related to someone from the house, as his last name is Grainger."

"As in Elize Grainger?" I asked, feeling prickles of tingles ripple up and down my arms and over my chest.

"No . . . was she part of the plantation owner's family? It's just that my husband thinks he's related to the servant boy that the house is

203

named after. In those days, servants often –"

"– took the plantation owners' names!" I finished her sentence.

I couldn't quite believe my luck. After the dead end of the mad, impossible, secret mission back in London, it was as if the god of coincidence was smiling down on me, giving me a great, big, enormous consolation prize. I mean, I was about to meet someone who was very possibly related to Joseph. . .

Suddenly, that ten-year-old boy whose life I'd tried to trace felt more real than it ever had when I'd looked into his eyes in the paintings and photos I'd seen, or even when I found his hidden-away gravestone.

"I can tell you *tons* of stuff about Joseph!" I burst out, bubbling over with enthusiasm. "And there's lots about him – and the old house – at the local museum!"

"No! Really? Wait till I tell – oh, here he is. Darling, we've had a bit of a stroke of luck!" said the woman, looking up at an older black man, in a matching rain jacket to hers.

The woman's husband seemed a little more hesitant and reserved than her, and didn't manage more than a polite smile before his wife started chattering again.

"This young lady – Stella, is it? – has some information about Joseph Grainger that I think you're going to find very interesting!"

I felt Mum wrap her arm around my shoulders and give me a squeeze, proud, I think, that I was able to be of such help to these strangers.

"There's even a bench in this park with a dedication to him!" I couldn't help jumping in and saying directly to the man with the tray.

He looked astonished, and plonked the tray of teas and cakes down unsteadily on the table.

"Did you hear that, Eddie? A bench! Right here!"

(Prickles and ripples.)

"Yes," said her husband, pulling out a chair and sitting down. "I h-h-heard. I'd l-l-love to see it!"

(Goosebumps upon goosebumps.)

It felt like *years* since I'd remembered to breathe, till I felt a pain in my chest, as well as a sharp jabbing in my upper arm from where Mum's fingernails were digging deep into my shoulders.

It was then that I knew she was thinking exactly the same thing.

It wasn't *just* that he was the right colour, the right *age*; it wasn't that his first name was the same, or that he had a soft stammer. It was the smile . . .

the broad smile with dimples, that looked instantly recognizable as the one in that precious 1960s photo, now taking pride of place on my shelves in my den back at the cottage.

"Mum," I said, in a voice slightly higher than normal. "Do you think it might be all right if they came round to ours, and I could show them all the newspaper articles I've got?"

Mum looked back at me, her eyes as wide as mine with possibilities, and didn't hesitate.

"Of course. *Definitely*," she said turning to the pleasantly surprised couple. "You'd be *more* than welcome to pop round for a cup of tea later, and have a look at all Stella's bits and pieces."

"Well, if it's no trouble!" the woman said delightedly, as her husband Eddie beamed his wonderfully new, wonderfully familiar smile our way.

Wow.

That wow was for this older guy sitting opposite as much as it was for us.

'Cause if he came around and happened to recognize himself in my prized photo, he might *just* find he'd discovered a whole branch *more* of his family tree than he'd ever expected to, on this trip to little, old, sleepy Portbay.

As I listened to Mum – who was trying her best

to carry on chatting casually – I stared hard at this sweet-faced man across from me, and tried to temper myself, to squash down any hopes that he was my grandad, just in case he wasn't.

Then I felt it – a soft, furry tail that I knew wasn't really there, winding its way soothingly around my legs.

And then I was certain.

Certain it was really him, Eddie.

Certain that if Eddie was related to Joseph, then it meant *I* was too.

And certain that coming to Portbay had been the most amazing thing to ever have happened to me.

I was suddenly sure as sure can be that the god of coincidences was actually nobody grand, but a spooky, fat, ginger cat that led me to this magical moment, from the very first time he'd purred at me.

Thanks, Peaches. . .

From: Frankie
To: *stella*
Subject: **Mind-blown and stupefied**

Hi, Stella!

Can't believe everything in that last attachment. Well, I *can* believe it, but it's left me mind-blown and stupefied. I just can't believe you found your grandad exactly where you weren't looking. OK, I *can*, 'cause we just had that whole conversation on the phone just now, when I finished reading your e-mail and you told me everything else.

But when you come in the Christmas holidays, are you going to have time to hang out with me, now that you've got a brand new grandad (and step-granny!) to visit? And will you even *want* to hang out with me, when I'm such a total muppet?

Sorry, sorry, sorry – I know I've never been very good at saying it, so I'm going to say it a lot now! I just didn't really understand till I read your attachment what I'd been like when you were here.

I can't say anything to excuse myself except that I was jealous (urgh!) and that I'm an idiot (obviously!) and that I'm sorry (again, times a million!).

Miss you ☹, but M8s 4eva ☺!*

Frankie xxx

PS I hope you like the photo I've attached – it was freezing the day me and Seb went to Victoria Park, and we had to ask a really grumpy woman to move over so we could get a good shot of the carving Eddie did. Hope you like it!

*And ever and ever and EVER!

Want to know more. . .?

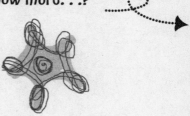

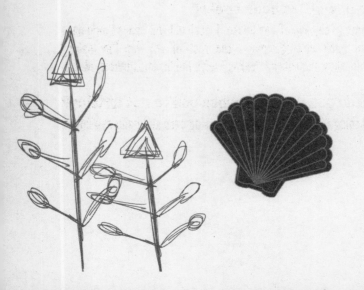

Meet the sparkly-gorgeous Karen McCombie!

★ **Describe yourself in five words. . .**

Scottish, confident, shy, calm, ditzy.

★ **How did you become an author-girl?**

When I was eight, my teacher Miss Thomson told me I should write a book one day. I forgot about that for (lots of) years, then when I was working on teen mags, I scribbled a few short stories for them and suddenly thought, "Hmmm, I'd love to try and write a book . . . can I?"

★ **Where do you write your books?**

In the loft room at the top of our house. I work v. hard 'cause I only have a little bit of book-writing time – the rest of the day I'm making Playdough dinosaurs or pretend "cafés" with my little daughter, Milly.

★ **What else do you get up to when you're not writing?**

Reading, watching DVDs, eating crisps, patting cats and belly dancing!

Look out for. . .

Dip into Rowan Love's secret diary, and discover her
sparkly, silly and seriously addictive world!

Six Words and a Wish

Karen McCombie

Surprises and spooks – nothing's straightforward
in Jem's world this Summer. . .

Check out Karen's super-cool website!

karenmccombie.com

For behind-the-scenes gossip on Karen's very own blog,
fab competitions and photo-galleries,
join her website of loveliness now!

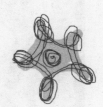